Ethan Wright

and the Curse of Silence

By

Kimbro West

Ethan Wright and the Curse of Silence

Young Adult Fiction

ISBN-13: 978-0-9887870-1-8

ISBN-10: 0-9887870-1-6

For Gerda

A special thanks to:

Chief Editor, Heidi Lunderberg

Cover and Book Art, Manthos Lappas

Reading Panel, Jody, Julie and Jordyn

Follow Author Kimbro West at:

www.kimbrowest.com

Contents

Ethan Wright

and the Curse of Silence

Gilfangir
Blackpeak Pass
Blackpeak Mountains
Kingspoint
Black Lake
Tirguard
Thomas River
Losalfar

Prelude

So who is Ethan Wright? He is but an idea, or a method of conclusion to be more specific. Maybe he is a weapon, or simply just a boy. Whatever he is, for the town of Whitehaven, he is a chosen saint... our chosen saint. It all stems from the creature, the one who has the ability to create and also take away. The Oroborus has the answers about Ethan Wright. The Oroborus has the answers about our future.

The tail devourer — you see, the Oroborus has a beginning, it has a middle and it has an end. It is a continuous circle of life. But Ethan Wright has only seen the beginning; he has not been given enough time. Time … it is a funny thing, meddlesome in appearance. When first perceived it has so many benefits — but when pondered, more drawbacks than anyone can ever imagine. The only thing a soul can truly own is their time — if you take that away … what is left? It is difficult for a King to ponder time ... I bet the alchemist knows.

I can only see myself lucky to be alive to witness this event. It is forbidden to interfere with the will of the Oroborus … forbidden to interfere with the Curse of Silence. But for this King to rule these lands, at this time, at just the right moment — I watch with an open mind, let the events unfold as intended and watch our saint discover who he is. This is my journal, the diary of a King.

King Basileus

A Brother Removed

Isaac staggered ... he paused as a drop of sweat formed at his brow from an exhausting battle. Blood dripped from his nose and trickled from his ears. He looked sick and pale as he knelt despairingly in the mud. With his head drooping, he leaned forward to reach for his sword. Before he could grasp the hilt, smoke plumed and swelled around him. And from the fog, a face formed. The mouth burst open as if to scream … but no sound came. The jaws stretched open as smoke roiled around Isaac, enveloping him. When the smoke dissipated, the bloody-nosed boy had disappeared….

Ethan awoke instantly. His breath came in jagged gasps as he jumped to his feet. His chest was pounding and he was covered in sweat, but the only thing he could think of was to find his brother in the darkness. He leaned over to his nightstand and lit an oil-soaked wick in an old lantern. As the small room was illuminated, Ethan looked to the opposite side. There stood the empty bed that once belonged to his twin brother. Ethan wiped his face with his bed sheets and peered across the room again; the bed was still empty. He let out a long, slow breath as he brushed his dark, messy hair out of his eyes. Realizing it was just another dream, he sat back down on his bed and rubbed his eyes. Was it possible that his brother was still alive? Was he at least safe somewhere? There was no way to know for sure.

Ethan noticed a slight movement out of the corner of his eye. He turned to see his grey-and-white cat Loki standing up and stretching at the foot of the bed. The cat looked annoyed from the sudden movement of the bed; he yawned and then looked at Ethan with his enormous green eyes. Ethan always thought the cat was a bit odd-looking, with flabby skin in his armpits and an extra toe on both of his front paws. He had been with the family since the birth of the twins and was always there for Ethan to draw comfort from. Tonight was no different from most nights. Loki jumped into Ethan's arms and presented him with an affectionate *meow*.

Ethan took the cat and walked through the dimly lit hallway into the study, where he found his favorite comfortable chair and sat down with a *plop*. The room was dark and dreary; there were old charts and maps strewn about the desk that had yellowed with age. As Ethan petted Loki, he noticed the coals in the fireplace still softly glowing.

"Another dream…?"

A frail voice came from across the room.

Ethan looked up, half-surprised his caretaker, Odin, was still awake. The withered-faced elder was sitting in a chair by the desk. Ethan went back to petting Loki.

"It's not bad to dream about your brother," the old caretaker said gently as he ran his long fingers through his silvery-grey hair. Odin rose, made his way to the kitchen, prepared some tea, and came back to the study.

"It's not that…." replied Ethan quietly.

"It does not mean you won't see him again. I am sure that wherever he is … he could be thinking of you right now — could be off somewhere having tea, just like we are."

He handed Ethan a steaming mug, which he grasped with both hands. The hot vapors were comforting on his face. Loki got up, annoyed, and jumped off Ethan's lap; he walked across the floor and curled up by the fireplace.

"It would be a nice thought, but somehow I don't think so," said Ethan. "I don't imagine him being the tea type."

"Oh, I see…." The old caretaker smiled. "I think there is more to dreams than you or I know."

When Ethan remained silent, Odin scratched his withering grey beard, leaned forward, picked up an old map off the desk and continued. "Your father made almost all of these maps, didn't he? It's rather amazing what some simple tools and the will to explore all over the countryside can do to an old man — don't you think?"

"I guess. But with such a poor memory I've never been able to figure out how he could document our front yard, let alone make a map of the entire city," replied Ethan smugly.

Odin snickered. "That may be true, but adventure … or misadventure — the spirit is in him, and I suspect Isaac has that same spirit."

"I know you would try and comfort me, Odin, but I know my brother well. He would not have left without saying anything."

"You may be right," replied Odin softly. He then paused and looked at Ethan with curiosity. "Tell me, what *did* you see in your dream this evening?"

The room went silent for a few moments. The glow from the fireplace glared off Ethan's face as he looked up at Odin.

"I saw the face again," replied Ethan blankly.

Odin nodded slightly, as if he was satisfied with the answer.

Ethan had recurring dreams about the fog attacking his twin. Although he was never used to the idea of seeing his brother in mortal turmoil, it did bring Ethan comfort to know that he could still visit his brother, even if it was in a dream.

Ethan gulped down his tea, grabbed Loki, and headed back to his bed to recover any sleep that remained while the stars blanketed the sky. He grabbed the covers that had fallen to the floor next to his bed and tossed them so they floated gracefully downward. Loki curled up at the foot of the bed and gave an affectionate *meow*, and Ethan closed his eyes and fell asleep.

The morning soon came and Ethan felt as refreshed as if he had gotten a full night's sleep. He rose to his feet and peered out the window. His friend Auren was already outside; Ethan threw his clothes on and ran out the front door. He skipped down half of the wooden stairs, grabbed the railing, and vaulted down the remainder of the staircase. He breathed in the fresh air of his hometown, Strahlung.

"Heya!" greeted Ethan. "You don't get up this early — where are you off to?"

"Father sent me off to the store to fetch some things," grumbled Auren. "He gets this way when Mum is on his case … you can run up with me if ya like."

Ethan nodded and the two began to amble down the small dirt trail that led to the small shop in the middle of town. The trail was just wide enough to pull a cart through, which Auren had done several times in the past to help the shopkeeper carry supplies. There were a series of wild-berried bushes to their left and tall pine trees to their right. They turned right at the next path that grew slightly wider and came upon the general store. They were met by a middle-aged man with very noticeable crow's-feet around his eyes.

"Good morning, Vincent," smiled Ethan.

"Ahh, good morning, just the two I wanted to see!" replied Vincent. He leaned down and put all the weight from his thin body into pushing a very heavy barrel up the ramp to the entrance of the store.

"Oh, let me get that for you," insisted Auren. He walked to the barrel, picked it up, and placed it on one of his shoulders. Auren was stockier than Ethan and always tried to impress his friends by showing off his strength. There was no doubt about it; he was indeed strong, and could lift more at the age of thirteen than most grown men.

"Oh thank you, Auren. My word, you are getting stronger, aren't you?"

Vincent motioned them into the front of the log structure and the three of them went inside.

"Age has its way of catching up with us. And as for my poor back, age has definitely caught up with me. You can set it down right here, Auren, thank you." The kind storekeeper rubbed the right side of his back with his hand while making his way to the other side of the counter. With a thud, Auren set down the barrel.

Vincent was now looking at the boys. "Now then, what can I do for you?"

"Just picking up some stuff for Father," replied Auren as he turned to peruse the store.

"Let me know if you need help finding anything." Vincent now focused his attention on Ethan. "So, any word from your father?"

"No, sir," replied Ethan quietly.

"Well, he is a mapmaker, right? Maybe he found some new territory to … ah — chart." Vincent was now scratching his slightly balding head.

"He has been gone for two years now."

"*Two years!* My my, the time certainly passes, doesn't it? Your father is known to have a terrible memory — could have got a bit turned around. But, it's like I always say — you can find your way into trouble easy, but getting out is twice as hard."

Auren was stumbling to the front counter with his hands full of goods for his father and some licorice root for the short trip back. He set the goods on the counter, pulled some money out of his pocket and handed it to the chatty storekeeper.

"So I suppose you two are entered in the youth sword competition tomorrow," said Vincent as he handed Auren his change. "I would think you two have a good chance to win this year, even with that pesky boy from Whitehaven. What was his name?"

"Marcus Grenwise," grated Auren while clenching his fists. "Man, that kid ticks me off!"

"Well at least you'll be there to teach him whose town is best, won't you now?" said Vincent sharply.

"No, actually," answered Auren.

"What do you mean, *no?*" grilled Vincent, who now seemed highly irritated.

"Well, Father says I am too big this year, and he doesn't want to risk me 'killing' one of the other entrants. I think it's Mum getting on his case about it — he was all about me entering last year," said Auren with a chuckle.

"But aren't you thirteen now? This is the last year you can enter.

Besides, I am closing my store just so I can go and watch you kick the tar out of those fellas!" exclaimed Vincent. "Well, what about you, Ethan? Surely *you* will enter this year."

"Well … no, I was never very good with a sword," replied Ethan.

"What? Your father was quite a good swordsman — hard to believe that some of his skill didn't rub off on you, eh?"

"Father always told Isaac and me that we would have to use our natural ability in the youth contests. He said it would be a better learning experience," answered Ethan, who was now staring at the floor.

"Natural ability, eh? Sounds like your father all right! Well then, say hello to Odin for me, and Auren, tell your father to reconsider. If anyone can defeat Marcus — well, I think you have a good shot."

The two boys said their goodbyes and headed out of the store with their licorice root in hand. As they walked, Ethan thought about the last time he fought in the youth sword competition. He had entered three years ago with his brother Isaac. Ethan had barely made it to the second round of the competition, and then lost immediately. Isaac, however, made it to the final match and then lost to Marcus Grenwise. That was the last night Ethan had ever seen his brother. He had always wondered if the competition was the reason Isaac left.

Auren took a piece of licorice root and snapped it in half,

handing the other half to Ethan. Auren started kicking a small rock; he would kick it up about ten paces and then kick it again while trying not to lose his pace. He kicked it again and it went to the left, in front of Ethan. Ethan was just about to continue the game when he overheard a familiar voice around the corner. It was Odin. He shot Auren a look, and they silently agreed to be sneaky and listen in.

"In my opinion, the General is a disgrace and in no way should he be leading their armies, let alone help run that disorganized place they call a city," said an unknown voice sternly.

"Well, you could be right. At any rate, we should investigate what he is up to before any action is taken," said Odin calmly. Odin had his cloak on and his hands tucked in front. He walked through town in no other way, and Ethan knew it was because one of his hands was partially crippled.

"I know I'm right, I have been watching him for years. He is no better than that father of his; always going on about his investments, or how much wealth their family has accumulated, or how no other is more successful than he and his precious son," rambled the strange man. He looked somewhat annoyed that Odin did not seem as perturbed as he was.

"Yes, indeed," smiled Odin. "I am more concerned that he may have a new friend that takes an interest in alchemy, much like our own Wegnel on the east side of town — most curious," said Odin with a raised brow.

"Wegnel? I would not go within a hundred feet of that lunatic."

Odin smiled gracefully. "Odd? Yes … but Wegnel is as harmless as you or I."

"That is *exactly* what I am afraid of," smirked the stranger.

He bowed slightly and put his hand atop Odin's covered hands, turned and departed. The boys began to duck behind the building, but it was too late; they had been spotted.

"Ahh, boys," smiled Odin. "And what are we up to on this fine morning?"

"Oh … nothing …" lied Ethan, "just bringing back Auren's shop list for his father."

"Yes sir, just picking some stuff up for my … er … father," repeated Auren.

"Ahh," smiled Odin, "carry on then, young masters."

"What do you think he meant by a loony alchemist on the east side?" asked Auren quietly, fearing Odin was still listening even from so great a distance.

"I don't know," said Ethan. "I've never heard of him speak of any kind of loony man, especially not a witch."

"Not a *witch* — an alchemist. They're into metals and herbal stuff. My father has spoken of alchemists, but I have never seen one," said Auren.

"Well, whatever he is — we should go check him out," Ethan said with a devious smile.

"Are you *mad?*" exclaimed Auren. "Why would we go and do that? That's all I need is for my father to find out I'm up to no good again — just got off the hook for that toad incident." He was speaking of when they had collected forty-two toads and set them free in Margret Tanbe's house.

"Well you can stay here if you want, but I'm going," said Ethan defiantly.

"Fine, I'll go, but let's at least wait until nightfall. It would be bad enough if we got caught, but sneaking around in the daytime is just *stupid*," replied Auren.

"Well then, I will meet you behind the store at nightfall," said Ethan.

Alchemy's Plump Cat

As night drew near, Ethan made his way out of the house. He skipped down the staircase and headed for the back of Vincent's store. The sun was now setting, and it was quiet throughout the neighborhood. He did not see any townsfolk out for a stroll, any kids playing with wooden swords in preparation for tomorrow's match, or any nosy neighbors poking their noses out of the softly lit windows. No, there was no sneaking involved. Ethan more or less had a casual walk down the dirt path that led to the old store and waited near some empty barrels for Auren. Soon enough, Auren came with a seemingly discouraged attitude.

"I still think this is a bad idea," said Auren insistently. This was not the first thing Ethan wanted to hear out of Auren's mouth. He thought about all the bad ideas Auren had come up with in the past, and how they would generally rush in without thought or care of the consequences. He thought that Auren may be reluctant to endure a possible scolding from his father, or worse, from his Mum.

"It's nice to see you too, Auren," said Ethan smartly.

"Okay then, can we just get this over with?"

They made their way through the night to the east side of town. As they walked, a fog started to settle in and a chill had worked its way down Ethan's spine.

"It feels strange over here," whispered Auren.

"What do you mean — you're not *scared* are you?" asked Ethan sarcastically.

"*No*, but something's not right — feels odd, is all."

The air seemed to get thick and Ethan's chest grew heavy. He started to realize what Auren was feeling. He wondered what they would do if someone jumped out and attacked them. At length, they came to a small wooded area covered in heavy fog that encased a small hut. Ethan could not believe that in such a small village, he had not discovered this place until now.

Suddenly, a loud howl came from the distance. Ethan could feel the hair on the back of his neck standing up. He quickly knelt down next to Auren, who had his finger over his lips.

"Shhh, did you hear that?" whispered Auren, looking from one side to the other, trying to determine the origin of the howl.

"What was it?" Ethan was slightly relieved that he was not hearing things but grew more alarmed at the thought of some creature getting closer to them.

"Shh!" prompted Auren. "It sounds like a wild boar."

A snorting sound was coming from the brush by the dwelling. The boys crept closer to the hut. It sat on short stilts, which made it appear to float in the dense fog. The roof was thatched with leaves and brush.

"Gnnuhhhh!" The noise appeared to be getting louder. "Gnnuuhhh … gnnwuaa …"

The boys reared up, and were given a start as the noise came from directly behind them. Auren fell forward on his face, and Ethan gave a slight gasp.

A chubby cat ambled its way through the brush; it leered at them and snorted. As it waddled toward them, Ethan could hear it gasping as if walking was an exhausting effort.

"Gave you a bit of a scare?" snickered Auren.

"And I suppose you fell down looking for licorice root?" Ethan retorted.

The fat cat gave them a filthy look and started to walk by. Suddenly it stopped with one front paw still in the air and looked just past them.

"WHO IS THERE?" came a shrieking voice. "I say, whoever is there, I warn you, I have a most ferocious animal here that will rip you to *shreds!*" The fat cat started rolling around in the dirt and continued snorting.

"*Gnnuhhhh.*"

Ethan realized the shrieking voice was referring to the chubby cat and he could not help but let out a chuckle. Just then a short old man approached the two boys who were on the ground. He was quite silly-looking in appearance; he was balding a bit, with tufts of grey hair sticking out here and there. His clothes were tattered and worn. His face seemed aged like a prune. And at the moment, he appeared exceedingly irritated.

The old man's wrinkles were bulging against his beady eyes as he approached the boys. "I say, are you laughing at my beast?" queried the odd-looking man.

"Well, he does look a bit silly," said Auren with a grin on his face.

"*She…*," corrected the old man, "…is one of the most *ferocious* felines in the land, I will have you know, and you can take that as a fact, because I said it is so, and so it is what I said it is. There are evil creatures about, but they never bother me because brave Ivy is out here protecting my dwelling — doubt that, would you? Such a small village and many strange faces coming through lately — here Ivy has caught you two, but you must not be strange folk since she has not *torn* you limb from limb!"

The two boys stared at each other blankly.

"You should feel very lucky just now I say," continued the old man. "Now come, come inside boys, before other dangerous creatures appear from the night."

He shooed them in the direction of the hut and they made their way inside. Ivy gave them a stare as the door closed, then the chubby feline continued to roll in the dirt and let out loud snorts.

The inside of the hut was cluttered with maps and strange glass containers — some of which appeared to be empty, and others that appeared to be full of partially congealing liquid. There were also some odd-looking mechanical devices sitting on a desk. They had a dull look to them and appeared to be half-way assembled, with parts and chunks of metal laying about.

"Cats … are one of the most powerful creatures around." The old man continued his speech without intermission. "They watch all, are commanded by none, and guard those whom matter most, and *most* is where and when the time that guarding is needed."

"You know," challenged Auren with a grin on his face, "she looks kinda fat and lazy to me."

"*Fat?*" argued the old man. "She eats what she kills, she does. You may think Ivy is *lazy* but mark my words," he got very quiet and serious, "cats are protectors of man and you will learn that before too long."

"Now then, my name is Wegnel the Alchemist and you may call me Wegnel the Alchemist. What is it that I can do for you?"

Ethan looked at Auren, and Auren back at Ethan. "Do for us, sir?" asked Ethan.

"Sir? Do you see a sir? You may address me as Wegnel the Alchemist." Wegnel paused and then continued, "yes yes, what do you need, you do not mean to tell me that you show up unscathed at my door with no need of *healing*, or age-implementing potion, turning ore into gold, or some kind of mathematical equation for solving the mysteries of the *universe?*" He looked surprised and somewhat riled up. "Ahh, maybe you came for something *more* then, yes maybe you came to see another plane of existence, to seek the challenge of the other side, to discover what it is and is not to dwell upon, for those questions that linger inside your head when you sit in the dark at your home, in your sleep, or in your dreams…."

Ethan was disturbed and Auren was beginning to look rather bored. "Uh, no thanks," said Ethan. "Actually, it's best if we get going now or Auren's father will certainly give us a reason to require healing."

Auren looked up. "Not to worry, Ethan, we're *fine.* Father said I can stay out *all night,*" he added with a smirk on his face.

Ethan knew Auren was exacting his revenge for being dragged out at his protest. Ethan shot him a look, and Auren continued to smile.

"What's the matter? Are you a non-believer in alchemy, that the twists and twines of the universe are solely derived to suit your needs, that the Norse and the Mitan and the Humans all live in one giant miscollaborated coincidence?" asked Wegnel mischievously.

"Ahh, we *really* must get going," said Ethan awkwardly.

He grabbed Auren and headed toward the door.

"Thanks for havin' us in then," said Ethan over his shoulder as they scurried out, past the fat cat and into the night.

"*Gnnnuuuuaaaa,*" snorted the cat as they disappeared into the fog.

The boys set off at a brisk pace in hopes of returning before Auren's father noticed he was gone.

"Well, Odin was right about one thing — Sir Wegnel the Alchemist is a loony," panted Ethan, partially out of breath.

"I thought he was brilliant," said Auren sarcastically.

Ethan sneered at him.

"Hey, *you* were the one who dragged me out tonight," shrugged Auren. "Now I'd better get running before my father finds out where we've been — gotta sneak back in the house."

Auren made his way straight home and Ethan started on his way as well. Unlike Auren, he had no father or mother to worry about him when he showed up late in the night. He missed having that, and thought about it often. Odin never got mad at him and sometimes encouraged his outings. Ethan made his way up the wooden staircase and inside the house. He found Odin waiting for him in the study.

"You met Wegnel I see," said Odin sternly.

"Wegnel the Alchemist … you mean," corrected Ethan.

"Indeed," replied Odin.

"How did you know…?" Ethan started to ask, but Odin interrupted him.

"I am not a useless old man, and this town has ears — that is for certain," said Odin. "Speaking of ears, I presume you heard me talking to Tothyll?"

"If you mean that strange man by the store, yes, I overheard you," replied Ethan hesitantly. He got a look from Odin. "I … I didn't mean to listen in on you, that is—"

"I have no doubt you meant well on your journey to Wegnel's place, which is why you will not be entering the youth sword competition tomorrow … and instead, you will help Wegnel with a task tomorrow night," said Odin calmly.

Although Ethan had no intention of entering the youth sword competition, he looked a bit surprised. He was not used to consequences occurring for his occasional wrongdoings. It reminded him of when his father and brother were around, and for once it made Ethan feel normal.

"Ah, yes sir…," replied Ethan. "If I may ask, what kind of task?"

"Collecting herbs for some kind of alchemy experiment for his newfound way to convert ore to gold I think," said Odin with a faint smile. "Ethan, I know you wanted to enter the competition—"

"I really don't care about the competition," replied Ethan quickly.

"Yes you do," answered Odin softly. "I want you to know that I am not doing this to be unfair to you."

There was a long silence before Ethan replied. "I know … goodnight, Odin, and … thanks."

Odin smiled and said goodnight. Ethan picked up Loki, who was already sleeping in front of the fire. He draped the cat over his shoulder and went to his room. He placed the cat at the foot of his bed. Loki got to his feet where he stretched, walked in a circle and plopped right back down.

"What do you think of all this, Loki?" whispered Ethan to his cat, who was now cleaning his face. "I don't think Father would care if I missed the sword competition — I know Isaac would, though." Ethan blew out the lantern and went to sleep knowing he had an interesting day ahead of him.

The Youth Sword Competition

Ethan awoke the next morning and joined Odin in the study with a cup of tea. Odin seemed distracted. He was concentrating his efforts on drawing a map while sipping from his almost-empty mug. Ethan noticed another, older-looking, map laying next to the one Odin was working on. He wondered why the old map was important enough for Odin to need a copy. Was it for tonight's task? The caretaker seemed so preoccupied with the details of the map that Ethan started to wonder if the old man had forgotten about last night, or the odd punishment that had been assigned. Ethan started to get up to leave when Odin spoke.

"I want you to take Loki with you tonight. I think it would be good to get him some exercise for a change."

"Okay," shrugged Ethan.

"And another thing," pestered Odin. "I found a package buried under some clutter. I am afraid my curiosity got the best of me, so I opened it and found this map, along with a note from your father."

Ethan took the old map and the note from Odin's grasp and read it aloud. "'Isaac, I finally found it, Thomas.'"

"What do you suppose he means … found what?" asked Ethan intently as he started to examine the map that Odin had been copying.

"I am not sure, Ethan. I figured he would want you to have it. I made a copy of it so I can do some research," said the caretaker as he put his head down and added the final touches to his copy.

Ethan grew frustrated as he studied the map. "*Tirguard?* What a stupid map, this place doesn't even *exist!*"

He started to pace back and forth while anger brewed in his eyes. "I bet he did go nuts, drawing up silly *maps*, and leaving his only family for *dead.* I hope he did go mad! He's much more trouble than he was ever worth anyway!" yelled Ethan as he cast the map into the smoldering fireplace.

Odin quickly retrieved the map from the fire. "Ethan, your

father…." But Ethan had already stomped out the front door with his wide-eyed grey and white cat trotting behind him.

Ethan tried to focus on the task he was to do that evening, but the events of the morning spun around in his head. He thought of the competition and how he would not be given a chance to face Marcus. He thought of his first encounter with Wegnel and pondered if he really was loony. But most of all, he thought of the old map, and imagined his father drawing it up for his missing brother. He wondered why his father would draw Isaac a map anyway. Maybe there would be a dotted line on the map that would lead him straight to his twin. He felt bad for yelling at his caretaker, and then decided it was good of Odin to have drawn a copy of it.

Ethan picked up Loki and held him up to his face. "What do you think? Do you think I screwed up?" He looked at the cat as if he was about to receive advice. "Oh, what am I thinking, I deserve to be punished," he said aloud.

It had been a long time since Ethan had received a punishment. He decided that he would do his best to help Wegnel so that Odin would hopefully look past his outburst from earlier that morning. But first, he decided to go on a small hike to Whitehaven and watch part of the youth sword competition.

"C'mon, Loki. Odin said we couldn't enter, but he didn't say anything about watching the first few matches."

The cat jumped down with a *plop* and followed Ethan toward Vincent's general store. There was a large wooden sign on the sturdy door that read '*Closed for Sword Competition*'.

Ethan chuckled. He continued walking, but then noticed the strange man that had been speaking to Odin now approaching.

"Greetings, Ethan. It is nice to see a young lad enjoying the day — shouldn't you be entered in the youth sword competition today?" asked the stranger abruptly.

He was very well dressed and carried himself with a strut that showed he was of higher society. He had a sneaky look on his face that made Ethan feel a bit uncomfortable. His hair was stiff and coarse with a dark silvery hue and even his shoes were of a high gloss that shone in the sunlight.

"I'm on my way there now," answered Ethan.

"A little late for signing up — don't you think?" asked the snooty gentleman.

Ethan nodded. "I'm just watching."

"Surely not, a young man with your skill would be in the fight, not on the sidelines. Besides, I was hoping to catch a glimpse of your skills with a sword, be it made of bamboo or whatever...." He pulled at the fingertips of his gloves, slid them into one of his pockets and then offered a hand to Ethan. Ethan paused, and then shook the man's hand. He tried to take his hand back, but was pulled in close.

"Do you know who I am, Ethan?" the silver-haired man asked quietly. As Ethan was pulled close he noticed the man had bright green eyes that seemed to peer right through his soul. Several necklaces and pendants clinked as he pulled Ethan forward. Ethan pulled his hand away and stood up tall.

"I saw you speaking with Odin. Your name is Tothyll."

"Yes, but more importantly is what I do — I am a recruiter for the Royal Guard. I was sent here for you … a Mr. Ethan Wright. I was hoping to catch a glimpse of you in this year's sword competition."

"Well it's too late to enter, so I'm going to go watch for a while. Please excuse me." Ethan started to walk around Tothyll, but was cut short.

"Being a man in my position, I have a certain pull with authority around here. Needless to say, I can easily get you into the next round of the competition. We will simply enter a bye for the first round, no problem. In return, I would ask that you simply consider the Guard—" insisted Tothyll.

"Not interested," said Ethan flatly as he walked around.

"One last thing — I heard news of you visiting Wegnel last night," challenged Tothyll.

Ethan stopped in his tracks. He had not told anyone, yet everyone seemed to know. Ethan smirked to himself as he thought of the babbling rambles that blurted unnecessarily from Wegnel's pruny face.

"Yeah, I met with him briefly," answered Ethan.

"Beware Wegnel the Alchemist — not to be trusted at all, young lad," said Tothyll smoothly. "I suppose a bright young boy like you saw right through his deceit, and I have full confidence you are not one to mingle with such foolish characters. I suspect a boy of your intelligence would have much better sense than that."

"Why do you care about Wegnel?"

Tothyll smiled and patted Ethan on the back.

"I don't … and neither should you. His reputation may get you into trouble — as a recruiter, protecting your reputation is extremely important to me," said Tothyll sincerely. He turned and started walking away. "Have a good time watching the tournament," he added.

Just then, Loki came trotting out from behind some empty barrels with a small rodent in his mouth. He set it down and licked his paws.

"We had better get started, Loki," said Ethan. They headed up the path toward Whitehaven. He thought about stopping at Auren's house, but decided to stay clear in case he was getting punished for last night. He continued on until he arrived at the busy city of Whitehaven. He had reached the giant wooden gate in just under an hour. The stone walls were decorated with dark blue and yellow banners, and several tents were set up outside the wide-open gate. People were bustling about. Some were selling food or youth competition swords and armor, and others were spectating or simply in the contest themselves.

Loki made a large leap onto Ethan's shoulders to escape the bustling crowd. Ethan began to make his way through the massive wooden gate of Whitehaven. The annual competition was the only time Ethan could remember the gate being wide open. As he walked further past the gate, he saw what appeared to be hundreds of young competitors dressed in leather armor and carrying two-handed bamboo swords. He could hear the loud *CRACK* of the bamboo echoing off the stone city walls. This competition was much larger than he remembered.

Suddenly, a couple broke through the crowd as their son was called up to fight. Ethan took a step backward to move out of their way, barging into the registration table. He quickly turned, causing Loki to dig his claws into Ethan's shoulders. Feeling the sting of the claws, Ethan put his hand on the cat to help him keep his balance.

"Hi there, can I help you with something?" said the young woman behind the registration table.

"Yeah," answered Ethan. "How many people have entered?"

"Almost three hundred — biggest year yet, I think. First one to get to three points is the winner — when quarter finals begin, it's the first to get to five, but who knows when that'll start — should run right into the night I'd say," answered the young woman.

Just then a voice announced two more names. "*Would John Fisher and Auren Faryndon report for a match.*"

"Thanks!" shouted Ethan as he turned and headed toward one of the empty rings, still holding onto Loki. He paused and peered around the audience to locate the evident commotion of the sword match that was about to begin. He spotted a larger boy wearing a leather vest and a padded helmet. As Ethan approached, he realized it was Auren, who seemed to be in a panic like he was looking for something.

"What are you doing here? I thought your father wouldn't let you enter the competition," interrogated Ethan.

"Yeah, well, what he doesn't know won't hurt anyone — I can't find my sword anywhere!" Auren seemed to be panic-stricken. He looked to his left and back to his right, then checked his pack, looked around the ground, and finally at Ethan.

"It's tied to your waist," replied Ethan.

"Oh, you could've said something," snapped Auren, now pulling the sword out of his belt and stalking into the would-be ring.

"Well *you* could have told your best friend that you were going to enter," spouted Ethan.

"Couldn't — didn't know 'til last night," answered Auren. But he saw that this did not seem to satisfy Ethan. "Aw, man, I had to enter — explain it to you after this fight — cheer for me, will ya?"

Ethan nodded.

Auren made his way to the middle of the ring, where his opponent was waiting for him. As soon as he got to the line the fight began and Auren was met with a barrage of attacks. He was able to clumsily block two of the attacks but was hit in the chest by a third. *Crack!*

A judge immediately chimed in. "*Fatal blow, two points!*"

"Fatal! C'mon, it was barely a scratch," protested Auren.

But his plea went unanswered and the judge chimed in again. "*Begin!*"

Auren was met with a similar barrage of attacks, but this time he was ready and counter-attacked, striking the boy's sword to the ground and then thrusting him in the chest.

"*One point awarded!*"

"So that one *wasn't* fatal then?" yelled Auren in protest again. He looked over at Ethan. "Can you believe this guy?"

The judge continued the match; this time Auren took the offensive and lunged at the boy. Auren was easily blocked, but then stepped past his opponent and slapped his sword on top of the boy's head, hitting his padded helmet.

"*Fatal blow, two points!*"

"Now that's more like it, judge! You and me, buddy!"

"*Your winner, Auren Faryndon.*"

Auren was so excited he almost jumped out of his shoes. He scrambled over to Ethan to give his impersonation of the match.

"Yeah yeah, I was here the whole time, remember?" said Ethan.

"Well yeah, but did you see how I finished him with that *spin* move?" said Auren exitedly.

"You didn't spin," replied Ethan.

"I did so," argued Auren.

"I didn't once see you spin," bickered Ethan.

"Probly cuz I'm lightning fast," answered Auren with a smile.

Auren started taking off his padded helmet. "So anyway, like I was saying — had to enter the competition."

"Why on earth would you *have* to enter?" challenged Ethan. "That doesn't make any sense at all!"

"It does so!" Auren started to look annoyed. "Look … last night I was on my way home when I ran into Marcus Grenwise and a bunch of his idiot friends — what they were doing in Strahlung, I have no idea. He started talkin' foul about you and your brother Isaac — said if he met either one of you in the contest today, that he would finish the job he started a few years back. Well, I knew you wouldn't enter, so I did. Thought someone should give that idiot a wallopin'!"

Ethan smiled. "Thanks."

"No problem really — well besides the fact that there are so many people here and the chances of me being matched up are—" Auren was cut off by the announcer.

"*Would Availia Tanbe and Marcus Grenwise report for a match.*"

"Looks like Marcus is up for a match right now," said Ethan.

Sure enough, Marcus and his followers shoved their way through the crowds of people. As he passed, he sneered at Ethan and Auren and stepped up to the line. His followers budged in front of Ethan and Auren, blocking their view. They reluctantly walked to the other side to cheer for Marcus' opponent. Ethan overheard some of the audience talking behind them. Marcus' opponent was an eleven-year-old girl. Neither of the boys had paid any attention to the name until they saw Margret Tanbe's little sister step into the ring. Ethan instantly thought of himself and Auren setting loose the forty-two toads in their house, and suddenly felt embarrassed by playing such a prank.

"It's Availia," exclaimed Auren.

"Yeah, Margret's little sister," replied Ethan.

Availia stretched out a bit, and with a strong voice let out a yell as she lunged forward with her bamboo sword. She had always been a bit smaller than the rest of the girls her age, but compared to Marcus, she was tiny.

"Don't think she'll fare well," stated Auren.

"I'm not too sure either," replied Ethan.

"*To the line*," declared the judge.

"Oh, a stupid little girl, eh?" snarled Marcus. "Don't you have some dollies to play with?" he taunted.

"*Begin*," yelled the judge.

Marcus immediately lunged forward and with all his might brought his sword down toward Availia's face. She lost her balance and was barely able to move out of the way, but avoided the blow. Marcus, however, was not impressed. He started to toy with her. He lunged forward a bit with his sword, missing on purpose to try and get a rise from the crowd. As soon as he took his eyes off her, Availia stepped forward, tapped his sword down with hers, and smacked the side of his face with her sword while giving out a yell. *Crack!*

"*Two points! Fatal blow.*"

Marcus bent over holding his ear, but quickly recovered and stood tall again. He seemed enraged and spat on the ground.

"Stupid girl, you should've stayed home with your dollies," he sneered, trying to get a reaction out of Availia, who remained silent.

Availia was studying Marcus' every move. Ethan guessed she was looking for a weakness, or simply hoping to get through the match without getting pummeled. And because Marcus was the returning champion, Ethan knew Availia had to perform her sword techniques perfectly in order to stand a chance.

"*To the line … begin!*"

Availia waited for Marcus to make the first move, and he did. He used his reach and lunged forward, hitting Availia square in the chest. *Crack!*

"*Fatal blow, two points!*" As the judge yelled, Ethan noticed a couple standing beside the ring, watching intently. One looked like a much taller version of Availia, who Ethan recognized as her mother. The parents looked very concerned for their daughter. After Availia absorbed the strike to the chest, her mother covered her face to avoid watching the display of brutality, whereupon she was comforted by her husband.

Availia regained her position and stepped forward to the line. She looked determined to beat Marcus and steadied her hands on the sword handle. The match was now drawing a fairly large crowd. Marcus, noticing the people gathering around the ring, stopped his barrage of insults in favor of concentrating on winning the match. He took a new stance and held the sword behind his back. He held it with his right hand so the blade ran up the middle of his back, but was hidden from Availia's view. Availia did not know what to make of the new stance and appeared to be ready to attack this time.

"To the line … begin!"

Availia immediately hopped forward and drove her sword straight toward Marcus' undefended face. It was too late. Marcus stepped to the side, spun around, whipped his sword around and engraved Availia's back, making a loud thumping sound.

Availia let out a gasp of air as she was hit, and fell to her knees. Marcus walked by her and paused. "Stupid little girl," he spat.

"*Fatal blow, two points — winner, Marcus Grenwise*," bellowed the judge.

Auren began to move toward Marcus to give him a piece of his mind, but Ethan grabbed his arm and held him in place as Availia's parents went into the ring to help up their now-crying daughter.

"What a *jerk!* Can you *believe* that guy? I mean *really*," Auren started yelling, which was drawing attention to himself.

"Yeah, he is a piece of work alright. I see why you entered," said Ethan.

"Yeah, but I may have to wait all day to get a chance to fight him — hope I can last that long, there are some pretty big thirteen-year-olds here. Almost like they keep gettin' bigger every year," replied Auren as a much larger boy walked by wearing a leather vest and cap.

"Oy — you there!" yelled Auren. The boy turned around and stared Auren in the face. "Are you in this competition? You *can't* be thirteen."

"Only twelve," replied the enormous boy as he turned and began to walk away.

"You see what I mean?" asked Auren, now looking at Ethan again. "I mean, what are they feeding these kids?"

"Don't know — probably best to focus on one match at a time though," replied Ethan.

"Good idea, hey — *you* should be my coach!" exclaimed Auren.

"Yeah, I can do that," replied Ethan, smiling. "You'd best be ready for them to call you up again — looks like they are trying to get these matches completed as fast as possible. The registration lady said there were too many entrants and it would run into the night. Then again, it'll probably be much later before you get paired up with Marcus."

Auren started to answer Ethan but was cut off by the announcer. "*Would Auren Faryndon and Marcus Grenwise report for a match.*"

A sick feeling came over Auren, and his face turned pale. He looked as if his stomach had just balled up and was going to come out of his mouth.

"Or maybe you'll get to fight him right away," said Ethan.

A Sore End

Knots were swirling and churning in the stomach of Auren Faryndon. His lips felt dry, his face was pale, and sweat rolled off his forehead. Auren picked up his helmet; the twitter of his nervous hands clumsily pulled it down atop his head.

"Strong as a bear, heart of a lion … strong as a bear, heart of a lion," whispered Auren to himself.

"Oh, you'll be alright, Auren, you're much bigger than him — think of how he treated Availia."

The color started returning to Auren's face. "You're right. I just need to relax so I can beat last year's returning champion, that's all then. Oh, why did I sign up for this again?"

But just then, Ethan heard a commotion over at the registration desk. It was Marcus.

"What do you mean I have to fight? I just got out of a match!" yelled Marcus to the besieged young lady. "This is so stupid — you wouldn't know how to run a …" but Marcus stopped himself as he noticed Ethan and Auren staring at him. "Fine, I don't need a rest anyway … to beat a big idiot like him!" He grabbed his sword and headed for the ring with his followers right behind him.

Ethan looked back at Auren and gave him a pat on the back. "Well, let's get on with it then … be precise — choose your spot and attack," encouraged Ethan as he gave Auren a thumbs up.

"Yeah … sure," answered Auren as he nervously stepped into the ring.

Ethan handed Auren his sword, and Strahlung's strongest champion strutted his way to the center of the ring.

"*To the line.*"

Marcus stepped up to the line, followed by Auren. "Not sure what all the gossip is about — you look like a big dumb oaf to me," taunted Marcus.

"I wonder, Marcus, did your rich parents pay those idiots to follow you around all day?" replied Auren sharply.

The face of Marcus Grenwise turned three shades of red as anger filled his eyes. "I'll teach you, Auren…."

"*Begin!*" yelled the judge.

Both boys lunged forward. Auren brought his sword above his head and swung wildly, as if to cut Marcus in half. Marcus stepped to the side, making Auren hit nothing but air. Auren's sword hit the ground, leaving him bent over. Marcus flicked his sword up and hit Auren full in the nose with a loud *CRACK!* Blood trickled out from Auren's nose and he held it shut with one hand, while trying to swing his sword with the other.

"*Hold! Unnecessary contact, no points will be awarded.*"

Auren wiped his bloody nose on the sleeve of his shirt, leaving a large stain on the already dingy material. He regained his composure and stepped back to the line.

"How did that feel, you dumb oaf — not so strong now, are you?" taunted Marcus.

"Ignore him, Auren!" yelled Ethan. "Be patient and wait for an opening!"

Auren nodded and got into position as Marcus continued to mock him. "Yeah, Auren, *ignore* him, you're too big and stupid to use your brain when you fight."

"*Begin!*"

This time Auren did not attack, letting Marcus jump forward. He wound up and swung for Auren's head, but Auren ducked, avoiding the swing. Marcus was now turned around, exposing his back. Auren took this opportunity to take a very hard swing, hitting Marcus square on the backside. The bully dropped his sword and reached around to hold his bottom, giving out a loud yelp.

"*Unnecessary contact! No points!*" yelled the judge.

The crowd was now laughing hysterically as last year's champion rubbed his stinging backside. Embarrassed, Marcus quickly snatched his sword from the ground and approached the line.

"I just wanted to show you what I thought of you," said Auren, chuckling. "What's the matter? Nothing to say?"

As Auren egged him on, Marcus went from embarrassed to angry. Auren got back in a ready stance and waited for the judge's signal.

"*To the line, begin!*"

The boys charged, swinging wildly, landing multiple strikes upon each other. The judge was not at all impressed and yelled for the boys to stop, but they did not. *Crack!* Marcus swung and landed a blow to Auren's shoulder; he ignored the sting and swung wildly back, hitting Marcus in the chest with a loud *thump!*

"*That's enough!*" yelled the judge.

Auren raised his sword again and swung hard at Marcus. He blocked the attack and the force broke Auren's sword in half. *Crack!*

"*Unnecessary, unnecessary, unnecessary!*" yelled the judge.

The boys backed off from each other. Both red-faced and gasping for breath, they turned to face the judge.

"*YOU TWO — WHAT KIND OF CONTEST DO YOU—*" The judge was livid. His face was turning red and he seemed to be at a loss for words.

Auren looked over at Ethan with his chest still heaving in and out from being winded. He shrugged his shoulders and looked back at the judge, who was now arguing with another official. The unknown official leaned in and whispered something in the judge's ear that appeared to be well received. He nodded and faced the boys to address them.

"*Auren Faryndon is to be disqualified and Marcus Grenwise will move on to the next round,*" announced the judge.

"*What?*" Auren lost his cool and started yelling. "What is this all about?" He started to approach the judge as Marcus and his followers started cheering.

Ethan began to run into the ring. Annoyed, Loki jumped off his shoulder and leaped on top of a small barrel sitting near the ring.

Ethan ran to Auren and grabbed him by the leather vest. "Let it go — you accomplished what you set out to do, let's just go," said Ethan as he got between Auren and the judge.

Auren realized what he was doing and tossed what was left of the broken sword on the ground. He turned and walked away, followed by Ethan.

"What a crock," protested Auren.

"Yeah, but you sure showed him — I mean, giving him a public spanking like that was genius!" exclaimed Ethan, smiling as he picked up Loki and started moving through the crowd.

"It was, wasn't it?" gloated Auren. "Hey, did you see that spin move I did?"

Ethan had still not seen this mysterious spin move. "Do we have to do this again? There was absolutely no spin move!"

Ethan, Auren and Loki left the large stone walls of Whitehaven behind and headed back to Strahlung. Ethan did not care who won the contest. Even if Auren did not get the best of last year's champion, Marcus seemed to do a good job of making a fool of himself. This brought great satisfaction to Ethan as he walked down the path that led to Auren's house.

"So what are you up to tonight?" asked Auren as they walked.

"Ah, I have to head home and talk to Odin, then it's off to serve my punishment for—" but Ethan was cut off by Auren's gloating.

"Ha! Told ya — *knew* you would get into trouble for the alchemist bit!"

Ethan took the gloating in stride. "Yeah, I don't mind it so much, just gotta go help Wegnel collect herbs or something."

"Wait, you gotta go *back?*" crowed Auren. "This just keeps getting better and better."

"Yeah, yeah," muttered Ethan. "Well then, see you tomorrow," he added as they reached Auren's house.

"Right, have fun with loony, I mean … Wegnel the Alchemist," winked Auren as he turned and headed for home.

Dendrobates Azureus

As Ethan skipped up the wooden staircase, he thought of what he would like to say to Odin. He knew he wanted to apologize for spouting off like he had. He thought about how much he looked up to Odin, considering him to be like family. As he walked into the study, he found Odin curled up with a blanket in front of the fireplace in his favorite chair, sleeping.

"Best not to bother you now," whispered Ethan. "Right then," he added as Odin let out a small twitch, followed by a nasal snoring sound.

Ethan snuck out of the room and headed to the porch. Loki was sitting by the stairs where Ethan had left him. He sat down next to the cat and started patting his head. As he pet Loki, Ethan started wondering about alchemy. He had grown up in this town, yet had never really spent much time on the east side. He knew it was desolate and forgotten about at times. Ethan was not really excited about spending time with Wegnel. He *was* interested in seeing what herbs and roots you could collect from the east side that you could not get from Vincent's store.

"You ready for some more exercise?"

The cat answered him with an affectionate *meow* and they both started toward Wegnel's hut. As they walked the air seemed to get thick and foggy, much like the last visit when he and Auren got caught by the fat snorting cat patrolling the area. Ethan and Loki headed through the fog and found a narrow trail that led directly to the hut. This was much better than the route he and Auren had tried to take the night before. When he came to the staircase, he was met with a familiar face.

"Oh, well, look who it is — get in trouble too did ya?" chuckled Ethan as Auren stood up from Wegnel's staircase.

"Mum saw the blood stains on my shirt and Father made me 'fess up," said Auren as he shrugged his shoulders. "Guess Odin told Father of your punishment — sent me to help. I guess it could've been a lot worse."

"Yeah, I don't think Odin was too fond of us sneaking around out here," replied Ethan.

"Well, let's get this over with," said Auren. "Oh, and told ya Wegnel's was a bad idea," he added.

"Yeah, yeah, and so was fighting in the contest," retorted Ethan.

"Nah … that was a *great* idea," exclaimed Auren as he started up the stairs.

"Yeah it was," said Ethan as he reached forward to knock.

Before the first rap hit the surface, the door pulled open to reveal a pruny face.

"Ahhhhhh, come come, we have much to do, let's get going, I see you have brought your cat, very wise, you have already begun to take Wegnel's advice. I see it as plain as the hair on your brow, you look as if you are ready to go."

Ethan and Auren stood with blank expressions as Wegnel leaned over and examined Loki. "Hmmmm, ahhhh, yes yes yes, a fine specimen, and what is this? Hmm."

He was looking over the same areas of Loki several times. He lifted Loki's paws and checked out his teeth thoroughly. Loki acted as if the examination were perfectly normal and cooperated, much to Ethan's surprise.

"Ahhh, he is an alpha, yes yes, I see you have a most interesting specimen here, yes, no doubt you are ready to go as well." Loki gave him a pleasing *meow* and lifted his chin. "Ah, excellent!" said Wegnel with a large grin." Time to go, much to do, much to do."

Ethan and Auren never made it inside, but swung around and started following the beady-eyed man. Wegnel went down the dilapidated steps and stopped abruptly at the bottom. Ethan almost ran into the back of him.

"Ivy, come come, it's time to go collecting!" The chubby cat came running out of the brush with her belly swinging back and forth and gave a proud snort as she sat down.

Wegnel looked down at his ferocious feline. "Play nice with Loki now," he stated while touching his finger to his nose. "He's an alpha," he added quietly, with a pleased look on his face.

"Uh, Wegnel the Alchemist, what's…?" Ethan started to ask, but was cut off.

"If I haven't said it a hundred times in all the stars, call me Wegnel, just Wegnel, my boy," he exclaimed.

"But yesterday—" whined Auren.

"What's this about yesterday? Today is anew, my boy, and I know nothing of what you speak, it is my name and I will have it spoken the same today as I have yesterday and the day preceding it," rambled Wegnel.

Ethan grew frustrated, but decided to drop it to avoid a long-winded and one-sided conversation of Wegnel arguing with himself.

"Wegnel, what exactly is an alpha?" asked Ethan, trying to change the subject.

"An alpha … why, an alpha is a descendant of great ancestry and if this fine animal were in a pack, he would most definitely be the leader of the lot. But more important is to get moving — don't want it too dark you see — a very small window to visit Dendrobates Azureus," replied Wegnel.

"Bless you," retorted Auren.

"What?" asked Ethan, ignoring Auren's comment.

"In some tongues it's the Venenum Spiculum, in others, the Dendrobates Azureus."

The boys stared at Wegnel blankly.

"You could just call it the Ravim, that is of course what the locals call the creature we are seeking," rambled Wegnel, lifting his eyebrows.

Auren did not say a word. He instead glanced at Ethan, who seemed a bit surprised. Neither one of the boys had expected to search for creatures; they had intended to gather roots or herbs. This relieved Ethan. If there was only a small window to catch the Ravim, then surely they would not be out all night.

Problems with Poison

The wind started to howl as cool air whipped by the alchemist's hut. A light misty rain began to fall as smaller droplets shot upward and whipped about. Ethan could see his breath and tucked his hands into his pockets to keep them warm.

"Here, boys. Take one of Wegnel's special torches, they are guaranteed not to go out, not in the rain or snow, and they burn extra bright. I have always carried one with me and you can always use a good torch if you ever find yourself wandering around at night."

Wegnel handed the boys each a metal rod with a small casing at the end. On top of the casing was an adjustable dial. He watched the boys spin the dials and stare at the special torches. Ethan looked over at Auren, shrugged his shoulders, and looked back to Wegnel.

"Well, give it a tap already!" said Wegnel impatiently. Ethan tapped it with his finger and nothing happened. Auren, on the other hand, tapped the end against a tree and a bright flame erupted from the end. Ethan followed suit and noticed that Wegnel seemed rather pleased with himself, and started to boast about his invention. As Wegnel continued to talk, the boys continued to try and ignore his ramblings.

They set off down the trail at a rather quick pace, with the cats following behind. When they reached the end of the trail, Wegnel continued into the forest, trudging through the thicket. Ethan could tell he had done this many times, for all the broken branches and twigs made it easier to get through. For an old man, Wegnel moved gracefully as the forest grew more and more dense. After an eternity of ducking under branches and hopping over downed trees, the boys started to wonder if they were getting turned around. However, Wegnel had finally stopped a few paces ahead. He turned and brought his finger to his lips, instructing the boys to stay quiet. Wegnel motioned with a free hand for Ethan and Auren to slowly approach. As they drew near, they were each handed a small brown satchel.

"What is this for?" whispered Ethan.

"Now, when he comes around I find the best thing to do is duck behind the trees and then … well, it's better if you just stay put this time," whispered Wegnel.

"Wegnel, what are we—"

At that very moment a handful of spikes stuck in the tree next to them. Ethan was given quite a start as he stared at the spikes embedded in the tree next to his face. He then promptly followed Wegnel's instructions and ducked behind the tree.

"Ivy, make for the Ravim, come on girl," wheedled Wegnel.

Ivy charged the Ravim and, surprisingly to Ethan, Loki also barreled toward the creature. Ethan could not resist taking a peek at the beast. Reared up on its stumpy legs, it was short and dark in color with a snout-like nose and sharp spikes sticking out from its well-armored back. It had a long, scaly tail with numerous smaller spikes protruding from the end. As the cats made their way around the Ravim, it launched several of the smaller spikes. Ethan noticed Wegnel gathering them in a brown satchel similar to the one that he was carrying. He exerted a small amount of force and pulled out one of the spikes from the tree next to him. Ethan thought how painful it would be to pull one from his own person.

Loki had the large beast cornered, and when the spikes would fling toward him he would leap up and over the creature. Ivy gave the Ravim a big enough target but still managed to gracefully move out of the way of any oncoming spikes. Suddenly, Loki stopped harassing the Ravim and turned with his ears perked up. He stared as a thunderous crash came from the woods. A large tree hit the ground, followed by another. Ethan looked up as branch after branch broke, and with a great thud a tree landed right next to him, making the ground shake. Just before the Ravim took its chance to escape, it launched a barrage of spikes at Loki, piercing the cat's hind leg with a small barb.

"Loki!" exclaimed Ethan as he ran over in a panic. All of this foolish gathering had wounded his cat.

"Watch out, Ethan," yelled Wegnel, "behind you!"

From behind, a towering beast approached, which Ethan could only assume was responsible for knocking over all the trees. The creature shoved its face through the thicket and glared at them through two big yellow eyes. At over ten feet tall, Ethan was sure this was not a Ravim, rather, a much more dangerous creature.

"Whoa, that is a big Ravim," exclaimed Auren.

"It's no Ravim," exclaimed Wegnel as he pushed Auren behind him. "It's a … lycanthrope … of sorts…."

"A what?"

"A werewolf … and … judging by his armored skin … a Stonewolf, I would say."

With stone-looking skin, tufts of fur, and old scars marking its body, the creature appeared to have been in many scraps previous to this encounter.

Ethan had never anything seen anything like it, but knew he was in significant danger. The beast was breathing heavily and drooling as it opened its gaping mouth and let out a terrible, deafening roar.

Ethan slowly stepped backward when he heard two loud bangs, followed by a billow of smoke at the Stonewolf's feet. Distracted, it stumbled and looked over at Wegnel, who was reaching for another exploding object from his pouch.

Loki seized the opportunity and charged the beast. He jumped onto one of the downed trees, launched himself at the Stonewolf's face and clawed one of its eyes. The beast flailed its arms, knocking the cat loose. As the grey and white alpha hit the ground, the Ravim's spike drove deeper into his leg. Loki gave a small yelp but managed to hobble over to Wegnel.

With a wounded eye, the Stonewolf regained its composure and took a step forward with one of its tree-trunk-sized legs. Wegnel threw more explosives at the beast, but they had no effect. Auren threw a large rock at the Stonewolf, which went unnoticed. The creature's focus was on the closest target to him; he was set on Ethan.

The Stonewolf charged Ethan at full speed, swinging its claws at

Ethan's head. Ethan ducked straightaway and the beast smashed the base of a tree. It let out another thunderous roar as it turned to view Ethan, who was now crawling over to where Wegnel and Auren stood. The Stonewolf started toward Ethan. Suddenly, the tree started splitting and snapping. The tree trunk cracked in half and came crashing down on the Stonewolf's leg and torso, pinning the beast down.

Ethan pushed himself off the ground and ran to Wegnel, where he was guided back to a safe distance.

"Hold on now fella, you will be of much more use without this lodged in you," said Wegnel as he bent down, pulling the spike out of Loki's leg.

Ethan bent down and tended to Loki while Wegnel, with spike in hand, grabbed several others and approached the Stonewolf. Wegnel put his best foot forward and jabbed the spikes into a soft spot on the Stonewolf's paw. He left them embedded in the creature's thick flesh.

Ethan noticed a giant iron cuff around the Stonewolf's ankle. It had odd-looking prongs that went upward and into the Stonewolf's flesh. It looked most painful.

Wegnel turned to the boys. "It's best we get going quickly, it will take a bit for the poison to slow down the likes of a lycanthrope of this nature."

"POISON?" yelled Ethan. "Those spikes are poisonous? But a spike was in Loki!"

"Yes, which is why we must act quickly — you need to carry Loki and do not let him move much for that will quicken the blood circulation it will — now move!" ordered Wegnel.

Worry poured over Ethan's body and was soon followed by adrenaline. He was worried about his cat's injury and doubted the loony alchemist, who had just put them in danger to begin with, would be able to help. Ethan thought it may be better to take Loki home and have Odin look at him, but before he could voice his protest they were running through the woods.

The night was pitch black. Ethan handed his torch to Auren but still found it difficult to maneuver around the broken branches while holding Loki. They reached the path and hurried back to the hut. When they arrived, Ivy lay down outside by the steps and let out a loud snort as Ethan followed Wegnel inside the dwelling. A small table was set up near the door. It had a small glass jar containing a thick green concoction. Ethan placed Loki on the table.

"Will he be alright?" asked Ethan intently. "I mean, you can fix him, right?"

Wegnel did not answer right away; he used a small knife to make a short incision where the spike had gone in. He squeezed the area and a clear substance leaked out. Wegnel then applied the green paste over the wound. Loki did not flinch and was very cooperative. Soon the leg was bandaged up and Wegnel gave him a pat on the head.

"He will be fine, he just needs to rest," said Wegnel. "Did you see, did you see what he did? That is an alpha if I ever saw one, my boy — yes indeed. Now then boys, how about some tea?"

Here's Pepper in Your Eye!

Ethan was relieved. His large-framed grey and white cat looked tired, but appeared to be in good spirits. Ethan sat down by Loki and sipped his tea while Auren took a seat in a big comfy chair. He looked as if he would pass out at any moment. Wegnel was looking over their collections from the evening. He took the spikes and placed them all in a leather pouch, along with some herbs. He rolled it up and fastened it shut with twine. He took a seat across from Ethan and prepared a pipe for himself.

"I know you have been through a lot this evening, but I need to ask a favor of you — I need you to deliver this pouch to me," said Wegnel.

"You … want me to … do *what?*" asked Ethan as he ran Wegnel's request through his head again, but remained confused.

"Well, I can't possibly take this and deliver it to myself, now, can I? How can I possibly know and expect myself to show up to receive the package while waiting for me to get here?"

Ethan thought this whole adventure had been a dangerous waste of time. Odin would be upset that Loki was injured, and Tothyll was probably right in saying Wegnel was not to be trusted. But how could he refuse — what would the alchemist have him do, take the satchel and give it right back?

"Sure, Wegnel, I can do that," said Ethan in a tired voice.

"You will, that's great, you are one heck of a lad Ethan, yes I knew as soon as Odin asked me to take you along with me that he saw something special in you, yes sir I told him that I did," spouted Wegnel in one long breath.

Wegnel took a couple puffs from his pipe, stood up and walked to the center of the room where there was an odd-looking chair. He removed the clutter from around it and placed it aside. There were straps on the chair that got Ethan curious as to what the alchemist was up to.

"Okay, my boy, jump in the chair and we will get you on your way," said Wegnel.

"On my way?" asked Ethan.

"Ahhh, you ask too many questions you do, it's not hard at all you see, you simply sit down in the chair and we can get you started on your journey to deliver this satchel to me, and then you can ask me all the questions you want."

Wegnel gave Ethan a small push toward the chair and Ethan sat down. Odin would not have sent him to a loony to get cooked on a spit with some herbs and a dash of seasoning, he thought. Wegnel fastened Ethan's arms down with the straps and presented a small vial of red powder.

"What are ya doin' to him?" Auren asked threateningly as he stood up.

"Calm down now, you're just like your father you are, with your short temper and such. Everything will be fine, just fine."

"So what now?" asked Ethan as he tested the tightness of the straps.

"Just relax," replied Wegnel. Then he dusted the powder in Ethan's eyes.

"AHH!" yelled Ethan. "What … is that … *pepper?*" He was panicking, but the straps held fast. "IT BURNS!"

"Well, yeah it's pepper, of sorts — ran out of the old stuff, I didn't really expect it to *burn*, really," replied Wegnel with a slightly puzzled look.

"Ahh, *I can't see a thing!*" exclaimed Ethan.

"Oh, perfect then," replied Wegnel, smiling.

Ethan felt a sting in his forearm, followed by a burning sensation. He fell backwards, his body twisting. He felt disoriented. Darkness came and went; he was falling through space and his mind grew dim. Ethan started feeling sick. Pressure was building up in his stomach as he fell and fell, until he could not bear it any longer … and then it stopped. Ethan opened his eyes to see a blurry figure standing over him.

"What …what just happened?" croaked Ethan.

"Well if I didn't see it with my own eyes," said a familiar voice. "Are you alright, Ethan?"

Ethan started to focus his eyes and saw Wegnel, but the old man was wearing different clothing. Ethan looked around and realized that the hut seemed to be decorated a bit differently as well.

Ethan wondered if he had passed out, or maybe this was all a very odd dream. "I'm alright," said Ethan. "I just feel a bit strange."

Ethan sat up and started taking a more detailed account of his surroundings. There were many devices on the shelves, none of which were taken apart, all of which seemed to be complete and new-looking. Another thing that caught his attention was that, for some reason, the sun was now up.

"Ahh, correct me if I'm wrong, but didn't we just fight a werewolf? And wasn't it nighttime? Where did Auren run off to? And didn't you just dump pepper in my eyes?" accused Ethan.

"Oh my, he is not still doing the pepper bit, is he?" asked Wegnel. "No, I don't recall fighting any werewolves with you and it has been daytime here for quite some time already."

Ethan grew more confused and rubbed his eyes. Realizing he was no longer strapped to the chair, he stood up quickly. "Loki!" exclaimed Ethan. He looked around for his cat, but the feline was nowhere to be found. Where there had been a table with green goop, there was now, in fact, no table at all.

"Loki…?" asked the old man.

"Yeah, uh … my cat," replied Ethan.

"Ahh, indeed he is," stated Wegnel. "I assure you he will be safe."

"But he was poisoned and I'm not sure—"

"Poisoned?" Wegnel cut him off. "Ah, then you have something for me."

Ethan realized the pouch was still attached to his waist. He untied it and handed it to the alchemist. Wegnel opened the pouch and removed the contents. He seemed very pleased. In fact, this meeting with Wegnel was nothing like Ethan's previous engagements with the man. Wegnel normally acted like a headcase, yet now, he was pleasant to speak with and seemed quite sane.

"Wegnel, can you tell me what exactly is going on?" asked Ethan.

"Yes, of course I can, but if you'd rather see for yourself, just step outside, and if you don't mind, please call me MacArthur," replied the the old man.

At this point Ethan did not care what the alchemist wanted his name to be; he just wanted to get out of there. He stood up, walked toward the door and pushed it open to peer outside. There were buildings lining the streets and high stone walls surrounding the city. Throngs of people were going about their business, smells of fresh fish and meat filled the air, and uniformed guards were stationed at different posts throughout the market.

Hesitantly, Ethan stepped down the rickety staircase of the hut and onto the street. Cobblestone formed a near-perfect pattern and was very pleasant to walk on.

Ethan looked directly across the street and saw an enormous shop. A huge sign hung over the entrance that read *'Lippy's'*. Another sign in the window read *'Home of the Lippy's Lickable Lightning Lemon Lollipops'*. Both sides of the hut were crowded with food vendors.

Some proprietors harassed passersby, while others had lines of impatient people.

In the distance, Ethan could see a lofty spire on the other side of a gate that led to the main part of the city. There was a small window near the top of the spire that would have a good view of the entire city.

He breathed in deep as smells of freshly cooked meat and spices filled his nose. Sweet desserts and freshly baked breads caught his eye. Pumpkin spice cakes with cream and fig, tart apple turnovers, and egg-whipped custard pudding were being sold from a booth right next to him.

Ethan was so intrigued by the delicious food in front of him that he did not notice many of the people had stopped to stare at him. And then it happened.

"Isaac…?" A guard left his post and approached from across the street. "Yeah, you look just like Isaac," he said, louder and more sure of himself.

Ethan felt a surge of excitement and he forgot all the questions that had been torturing him about where he was.

"Isaac, you know Isaac?" asked Ethan frantically.

The guard scratched his head. "Well, you're not him — you look rather young to be Isaac Wright. You his little brother or somethin'?"

"So you're saying you know Isaac Wright?"

"Of course I know him. Who *hasn't* heard of Isaac Wright?"

Ethan looked confused, but remained hopeful. "I'm his twin brother, Ethan. I have been searching for him — you know where I can find him?"

"Haven't seen him in ages … maybe ten years…." answered the guard.

Ethan was bewildered. For three years he had waited to hear news of his missing brother. Now, a man recognizes Ethan and says he has not seen Isaac for *ten years*. Ethan thought the guard must be either crazy or mistaken.

"Um … thanks then," mumbled Ethan disappointedly.

Ethan turned and climbed the stairs that led back into the hut. He was both angry and confused, feeling he had been tricked somehow. Having a look around had not cleared things up at all. Not only did he have no idea what was going on, he had no idea where he was *or* how he had gotten there.

"WHAT IS THIS ALL ABOUT?" demanded Ethan. He caught his breath momentarily and then quietly asked, "where am I?"

"You are in the spectacular stone city of Tirguard."

"Tirguard," Ethan whispered to himself. He knew he had heard that name somewhere before.

"Well, you had better have a seat and I will explain everything," said MacArthur calmly as he filled his mouth with cake that Ethan recognized from one of the street vendors. "Pumpkin spice cake?" he offered.

Ethan shook his head.

"Do you mind if I?" asked MacArthur as he piled the rest of the cake in his mouth.

Ethan ignored the question and had a seat in a comfy-looking chair. MacArthur poured Ethan some tea and then walked over to a large wooden chest with metal workings on the front. It was quite a beautiful piece of furniture. He pulled from it a silk bag that he set down on the table with the utmost delicacy. MacArthur opened the bag and pulled out a scaly snake-like creature. It was rather an odd-looking creature with a dragon-like head, no arms and no legs. The creature was blue and scaly with a black belly that had a peculiar design all the way to its chin. It was in a circle and remained so, because its tail was wedged firmly inside its mouth. The creature's fangs were inserted into its own body.

Ethan sat up in his chair and marveled at the odd-looking reptile. "What is *that?*" he asked curiously.

He was quickly answered. "He's an Oroborus, Ethan — very rare creature indeed. In fact, he is one of only two that I know of. And, I have not heard anything of this one's brother for a few years now. But then again, I don't get out of the hut much," smiled the alchemist.

He set the Oroborus down on top of the silk bag and sat down across from Ethan. They sipped their tea. The creature slid back its nearly invisible eyelids, revealing black eyes that appeared infinite. It was staring right at Ethan, and for a moment, Ethan felt he could not look away.

"You see, Ethan, this is how you got here. The place in which you come from has a Wegnel, correct? This place also has a Wegnel, which is why I would have you call *me* by my surname, MacArthur," explained MacArthur.

Ethan nodded.

"The *other* Wegnel has been known to give a distraction because some people fear getting bitten by a creature such as this," said MacArthur calmly.

"THAT THING BIT ME?" asked Ethan in a panic.

"Yes, he certainly did. Right there on your forearm," replied MacArthur.

Ethan looked down and grabbed his forearm, which did not look like it had been bitten at all. "But there is no mark—"

"No, and there wouldn't be," interrupted MacArthur. "You see, the Oroborus is said to be the first creature in existence. He is so perfect that he does not need to eat food, breathe air, or have any senses at all. However, he has been known to get rather curious from time to time."

MacArthur looked over to the Oroborus, who now had closed eyelids.

"How does it survive without food?" asked Ethan.

"Well as you can see he devours his own tail, but is constantly growing at the same time. He is self-sufficient," replied MacArthur. "And there is something else that is very special about Dimon—"

"Dimon?"

"Well, he's got to have a name, doesn't he?" chuckled MacArthur. "As I was saying, Dimon can send someone from one world to the next — a parallel universe, another dimension, whatever you wish to call it. But the history of these creatures reveals that there are seven different worlds in the galaxy that are meant for men to explore. They are called Athani, Alfhemir, Enterom, Esurio, Inhalo, Prodigo, and Contabesco — you're in Alfhemir and came from Enterom … god forbid you ever have to go to Contabesco…."

"Ah, ahh…," stuttered Ethan. "I think there's been some kind of mistake here — first off, I haven't heard of any of those places. Secondly, you've got a giant snake in your kitchen … what I mean to say … is … well I'm not entirely sure what I want to say. I haven't been sure about anything since the moment I met you … both times."

"I understand," said MacArthur calmly. "That's why I drugged your tea."

"YOU *WHAT?*"

"Hold on now," soothed MacArthur.

"WHAT IS *WRONG* WITH YOU?" exclaimed Ethan.

"In my defense, I could tell that you were going to panic. You will have about five minutes before you pass out. So you can either pass out in this hut, or out on the street in a strange world. Either way I will get you back in this chair," said MacArthur as he held the back of the chair that Ethan had been strapped to earlier.

Ethan considered for a moment and then caught his breath. "So what now?" he muttered.

"Well, you can take advantage of the next five minutes and find out more about where you are and why you are here ... or ... you can panic."

Ethan thought for a moment, folded his arms in front of him, and then unfolded them.

"Can I get back?" he asked.

"Of course you can. Most of the people here use the Oroborus to move between these two planes of existence. But you must be very careful. Spend many years here — go back, and just a few weeks may have passed. Time and space work much differently between all places," explained MacArthur.

"So who is Wegnel at my home, in Enterom?" asked Ethan, who was now pretending to play along.

"He is me. I have spent many years training in alchemy, and have bonded with the Oroborus. Only an alchemist could survive such a feat. If any other *tried* they may succeed for a short time — but a lifetime here in Alfhemir is only a few years in Enterom. And when one of us dies, we *both* will die. That is what the ingredients in the pouch you brought me are for. With these, I can create an elixir that extends my life so Wegnel and I can act as a gateway between the two worlds. You see, I am nearly seven hundred years old, but I don't think I look a day older than sixty-five. Not too shabby I think — not too bad at all," said MacArthur, looking rather pleased with himself.

Ethan thought for a second that he might be going crazy. Maybe he had been drugged long before he drank MacArthur's tea. Or he could have been knocked out and dragged into the woods of Strahlung by the crazy old man, and this was all just a dream. But then he remembered Auren — and knew his friend would have prevented anything from happening. He reluctantly accepted the alchemist's explanation for now.

MacArthur unpacked the pouch of poisonous spikes and herbs. He grabbed some other ingredients from a shelf. He placed all the items on the table next to a device that looked similar to a clock. It had funny-looking silver hands that moved horizontally. Other symbols lined up when the hands were in proper position. Ethan had never seen a clock quite like it. He watched MacArthur as he opened a door on the back of the clock and stuffed the ingredients inside.

"What are you doing?" asked Ethan as he leaned forward to see the back of the clock.

"Well, I am placing the items in the clock so they do not age," answered MacArthur precisely.

Ethan was hopelessly confused. "What exactly do you mean?" he asked.

"It's an old alchemy wives' tale, Ethan." MacArthur sat up a bit taller as he began to recite, "'"in the clock will save you from time, the ageless items you will store, and age will bother you no more."' And with that, MacArthur latched the back of the clock closed and smiled at Ethan. "If you ask me it's a bunch of nonsense, but storing an anti-aging elixer in a clock has a bit of poetry to it, I suppose," he added.

"So let me get this straight…," said Ethan. "I was in a place called —"

MacArthur immediately filled in the blank. "Enterom…."

"Yeah, in Enterom — an alchemist named Wegnel, which is you, threw pepper in my eyes — then I was bit by a snake thing, that is an Oroborus named Dimon, which sent me to another world named Alfhemir, in a city called Tirguard, where I find you … who is Wegnel, but wants to be called MacArthur and offer me pumpkin spice cake?" spouted Ethan, who then stopped to take a breath.

"And?" challenged MacArthur.

"And what?"

MacArthur stood up and moved his now-empty mug onto the table and looked at Ethan. "And now we should probably get you back," he said. "We don't want anyone getting worried about you."

"Worried about me? People should be worried … I've been drugged!" exclaimed Ethan.

"No you weren't, Ethan. I just said that so you'd hear me out. Most people panic and run out to the streets before listening to the whole explanation. Then I have to go and track them down, and by that time—"

"Wait, so you *haven't* drugged me?"

"Wegnel has his tricks and I have mine. It's been over five minutes … do you feel like you're going to pass out?"

Ethan thought for a moment and then shook his head.

MacArthur motioned him over to the chair. Ethan sat down once again. Dimon was brought over to Ethan, and the Oroborus slowly removed its fangs from its tail. Ethan was expecting to see a chewed-up nub, but instead was presented with an array of colors on a plume-shaped tail. Dimon quickly sank his teeth into Ethan's arm; he did not have time to resist or flinch.

"Waking, sleeping, dreaming…," he heard MacArthur whisper. "I will see you again soon … Ethan Wright."

Ethan winced from the sting and entered into darkness again. Time took him. He felt as if he was falling again. Much like last time, as soon as he could not bear it anymore, he awoke.

Ethan once again felt groggy. He glanced around and realized he was in the old hut with the devices that were half taken apart. He looked to the window and it was nighttime again. He saw Loki on the table, licking his wound. Auren was sitting in the comfy chair, starting to doze off. Realizing that Ethan had returned, he jumped with a snort.

"Ethan! You're back — you okay? That was *so* wild, if you didn't show up I was gonna have ol' Wegnel's neck!"

"Yeah, I'm okay … I'm just a bit tired actually; we must have been out almost all night," replied Ethan.

Auren looked at him, confused. "Ah … you've only been gone for maybe … five minutes — you sure you're okay?"

"Yeah, I feel okay, where's Wegnel?" asked Ethan.

Just then, Wegnel came in with his tattered clothing on and his tufts of hair all about. He looked much different than his other self, indeed. Wegnel spotted Ethan and smiled.

"So you delivered the satchel then, and how did I look? Well I presume, I always hear that I look in much better shape than myself, and I always say that it is because I take such good care of myself and if it were not for me we would both be dead. I always say if he doesn't stop being so loony all the time he's going to find himself decapitated. Where do you think that would leave me? I'll tell you where that would leave me, losing all my marbles that's where," babbled Wegnel in his normal long-winded conversation with himself.

"It went fine … Wegnel," replied Ethan.

"I knew it would, Ethan," smiled Wegnel.

Auren looked up quickly and said, "Don't you mean *Wegnel the Alchemist?*"

Ethan looked at him and shook his head, letting Auren know he should drop the subject. For some unknown reason, Wegnel ignored Auren's comment. He continued rambling about how much better-looking he was than his other self.

"Well, you boys better get going then. Ethan, I will keep Loki here tonight and bring him over tomorrow morning — best if he rests up for now. Fighting lycanthrope is not an easy business you know — having slain many before, Ivy likes to rest afterwards for a day or so," rambled Wegnel.

"Maybe after she *ate* a lycanthrope…." muttered Auren.

Wegnel shot Auren a dirty look, and the boys took this as their sign to leave. Ethan gave Loki some affection before exiting. Loki nodded his head, letting Ethan know he would be fine. The two boys left the hut and headed home.

Green Goop

That night Ethan lay awake in bed thinking about his experience at Wegnel's hut. Unable to sleep, he lit the lantern and noticed the old map rolled up on his nightstand. He unrolled it and began to study it carefully. He realized that it had no burn or scorch marks, yet he recognized it as the original and not the copy that Odin had hastily made. As he moved his eyes down the map, he spotted a familiar name.

"Tirguard," he said to himself quietly. "MacArthur was telling the truth … but this doesn't make any sense."

He continued his perusal. There was a large '*M*' on the map, with a depiction of an Oroborus forming a circle around the '*M*', and arrows pointing up and down. The top arrow had a large '*N*', and the bottom had a much smaller '*n*'. Ethan thought this must be a mistake, as the bottom should read 'south'. Tirguard was near the center of the map. To the north was a city named Losalfar, and to the northeast was a city called Gilfangir.

There were several other cities on the map, but Ethan was too tired to investigate further. The flicker of the lantern sent shadows of Ethan's messy hair onto the map. He brushed back his hair and got comfy. He missed the grey and white cat at his feet, and there was still no brother in the bed across from his own. While in Tirguard, Ethan had felt closer to his brother than he had in a long time, though Isaac was still nowhere to be seen. Ethan yawned. His eyes grew heavy and he drifted to sleep with the map clenched in his hands.

A massive pressure surge ripped through Isaac, sending him to the ground in agony. A drop of sweat formed at his brow from an exhausting battle. Blood dripped from his nose and trickled from his ears. He knelt despairingly in the mud. With his head drooping, he saw his reflection in a small mud puddle, revealing a tired, pale-faced boy. A sword lay half-covered in mud a couple feet from him. He leaned forward to reach for it. Before he could grasp the hilt, he

noticed his reflection had dissipated and was replaced by a small object shining in the puddle. Isaac reached down to pick it up. As he did, smoke plumed and swelled around him, forming a face whose jaws stretched open, enveloping him.

Ethan bolted upright, covered in sweat. He was becoming more familiar with the dreams now and knew he would not get back to sleep. But this time, he did not have to. The sun was peeking through his window, letting him know it was morning. This dream made it further than the others. Ethan wondered if it meant anything. Maybe it meant he was supposed to do something, or maybe it meant absolutely nothing. He could never grasp why this dream in particular jogged through his mind so much. He had often wondered if it were real. One thing he *did* know is that the dream, whether it was good or bad, gave him a glimpse of his brother, which brought him comfort. That would have to be good enough for now.

Ethan jumped out of bed with a much more focused outlook on the day. He got dressed, stuffed the map in his pocket and went to the study expecting to see Odin, who was not there.

"Odin!" yelled Ethan, but no answer came. He went into the kitchen and started making tea. He preferred licorice tea which reminded him of his brother. When they had gone exploring, they would often chew on licorice root, as he and Auren did now. He finished making the tea and went to the study. He noticed a note on the desk before he sat down.

"*Ethan, went to run errands — will return tomorrow — Odin.*"

Since Ethan had not checked the desk last night, he was now wondering if Odin left yesterday or earlier this morning. Ethan decided he would just wait for Odin. Since he was expecting Wegnel to show up with his cat, maybe he could get some answers from *both* of them regarding Tirguard.

Ethan started to get restless as the day wore on. He sat on the front porch to enjoy some of the day. He pulled the map out and started to study it again. Soon, he noticed Wegnel walking down the path toward his house. He shoved the map in his pocket and stood up to greet the alchemist. He saw a chubby feline trailing behind Wegnel; the cat was grunting and snorting as usual. Her belly waddled back and forth as she made her way. Wegnel was carrying Loki in a small partially-open satchel.

"Hello there, Ethan!" greeted Wegnel with a smile. "Wonderful day, simply magnificent I say, and I should know how well the day has been going because I have been enjoying it since I woke up this morning."

"Hey Wegnel, nice to see you," replied Ethan.

"Here is a special young patient I have for you," said Wegnel. "He is doing fine fine, he is already trying to walk, and a strong one he is. I have to say, I am rather impressed by this one."

Loki looked tired, but was content to be with his owner again. Ethan took Loki from the satchel and held him in his lap. The wound looked much better now that it was clean. Wegnel's green mystery goop was pasted about the area. Loki rested his head on Ethan's lap and closed his eyes.

"He is very tired, but he'll be fine, fine I say, he is very strong indeed," said Wegnel.

"Thank you for taking care of him," said Ethan with a smile. "He helped save me in the forest … you helped save me in the forest … thank you … Wegnel."

For once Wegnel did not speak. He blushed a bit and flapped his hand, as if to say it was no big deal.

"Do you want some tea?" asked Ethan.

"Oh yes, don't mind if I do. Thank you very much," replied Wegnel gratefully.

Ethan brought Loki inside and put him down on a blanket in the study. Loki nodded his head, tucked it back down, and went to sleep. Ethan brought two mugs of tea outside for Wegnel and himself. Wegnel took the mug and held it under his nose.

"Ah, this smells familiar it does, licorice is it? Yes I recognize this from many years ago. Good stuff this is."

Wegnel breathed in the aroma from the mug and took a sip. Ethan was trying to work up courage to ask Wegnel some questions about what he had seen the night before.

"Wegnel, have you ever been to Tirguard?" asked Ethan.

"Oh yes yes yes … technically … I'm there right now … aren't I? I mean … I think I am … or maybe not so much … hmm…." said Wegnel, with his nose still buried in the mug. He looked up at Ethan. "Well then, out with it, why do you ask? Maybe you are just curious or maybe you ask for another reason?"

"Well, it's just that … I met a guard that mistook me for someone else — someone very close to me … my brother, Isaac."

"Your twin brother if I'm not mistaken, am I? Yes, yes," said Wegnel. "Do you know why the guard mistook you for your brother?"

Before Ethan could speak, Wegnel provided the answer. "Because … your brother was in Tirguard, and he became rather important. Your brother was very important indeed. He had many adventures and saved the city more than once you know. And I say this because I was there, and sent myself word on it often," said Wegnel.

Ethan looked up at Wegnel. "Do you know if he's still there? I mean, can I go and see him?"

"You will see him again indeed," said Wegnel, looking up from his mug.

Ethan looked at him in disbelief. He had asked many people in Strahlung if they knew the whereabouts of his twin brother, and all this time he just had to ask the alchemist. He wondered how the alchemist knew Ethan would see Isaac again.

Suddenly a wagon approached. Ethan and Wegnel stood up to get a better look. The wagon was slowly being pulled by a massive dark brown horse. There were two men walking next to the horse, guiding it up toward the house.

"He was hurt, I'm afraid," yelled the first man as they approached.

"WHAT?" bellowed Ethan.

"Odin … your master, he was hurt a bit — he'll be fine though," said the man.

The second man helped Odin out of the wagon. It seemed Odin could walk just fine under his own power.

"I'm fine, I'm fine," groused Odin. "I don't need anyone making any fuss over me — I can handle myself just fine."

"He's very stubborn," said the second man as he got the wagon turned around.

Odin was wearing a cloak with the hood pulled up. The caretaker climbed the staircase, giving Ethan a good look at his injury. Odin had a gash that ran down the length of his face. The gash seemed to have been made by a large claw, with a second gouge down his ear and jaw that was meager in comparison. Dried blood was smeared down the side of his face from someone's attempt to clean the wound.

Odin smiled at Ethan. "Oh, I have had much worse than this, I assure you. I will be quite alright."

Ethan looked at him. "How did this happen?"

"Let me get some herbs on that wound and we can go over the details we can, this will be no problem indeed, I can have you patched up in a minute," said Wegnel as he reached inside his satchel.

Odin smiled as Ethan helped him up the stairs and into the chair on the front porch.

"Thank you, my friends."

Wegnel spent the next few moments mixing his ingredients and applying the resulting green goop to Odin's face.

"It seems a giant werewolf was loose, roaming about. My curiosity must have gotten the best of me," said Odin.

"We ran into a lycanthrope last night…." said Wegnel. "Or at least a very large stone with a severe lycanthropic condition."

"Indeed, I saw the poison spikes in its foot. If it weren't for that, and of course that it seemed half blind, I'm afraid it would have been difficult for me to escape … mostly intact…." replied Odin woefully. He looked at Ethan with a concerned expression. "You were very lucky to have survived such an encounter."

"As are you, Odin."

"Rest rest, Odin needs to rest now, and I need to be on my way." Wegnel gathered his remaining supplies and set the small jar of green mystery paste on the table. "Put some more of this on both Odin and Loki tonight and make sure they get plenty of rest — that's a good lad, bring them by tomorrow for a checkup," he added.

Ethan nodded. He wanted to ask more questions of the alchemist, but decided he had enough to worry about, what with taking care of his cat and Odin.

A Trip Through Time

The day's affairs came to order quickly the next morning. Odin, ignoring his get-rest orders from Wegnel, was up very early. He was drinking tea and making a bustling racket which woke Ethan up. Grappling with the idea of getting out of bed, Ethan pushed the sheets off his face. He was rather glad to see the six-toed cat was again at the foot of his bed, looking as if he were ready to go back to his day-to-day routine. Ethan gave him some attention and then proceeded into the study to look for Odin. He found his caretaker going through shelves that had lacked the organizational aspect of any well-respected mapmaker. He had stirred up quite a bit of dust and was mumbling about the map he had discovered the other day.

"Ah…." Odin looked up at Ethan while holding up a backpack. "Here it has been all along; it is always in the last place you look, but also the last place you expect to find it," he said with a hint of excitement.

It was raining lightly that morning and thunder was rolling in the distance. It did not seem that the rain would let up any time soon and Ethan was starting to wonder if the weather was affecting Odin's mind.

"Shouldn't you be resting?" asked Ethan.

"Nonsense my boy, now get your things packed up, we must get going before the storm gets worse," replied Odin.

Ethan looked surprised. "Odin, what do you mean — Wegnel's … already? What are you up to?"

"Always up to no good I'm afraid," Odin said with a wink of his eye. "We are going to Ghislain's."

"Auren's father — but … what for?" said Ethan, now wondering if he was to be punished for some additional crime that he was unaware of.

"We have business," stated Odin. He had already filled his pack with several items — he looked as if he were ready to be gone for a week.

Ethan shrugged his shoulders, downed a mug of tea that Odin

had made, and then grabbed his map and the miracle torch that he had received from Wegnel. He stuffed the items in his pockets and walked into the study.

"I'm ready, Odin."

"Good," smiled Odin, flinging the pack over his shoulder.

They made their way out the front door and down the trail. They walked briskly to avoid getting soaked. A quickened pace did not seem to help them, for the rain started coming down heavily and they found themselves drenched.

"Well this is mighty fine," muttered Ethan.

"No matter now, we are almost there!"

They passed Vincent's store and pushed farther down the trail until they arrived at Auren's house. It was a sturdy-looking stone house built into the side of a very tall hill. It had a very comfortable appearance to it and smoke was billowing from the chimney. They rapped on the door and were greeted immediately by Ghislain. Auren was standing behind his father with a welcoming look on his face.

"Odin!" exclaimed Ghislain with a welcoming smile on his face. This surprised Ethan because in his previous encounters with Ghislain, Auren's father had never looked particularly approachable. "Come inside out of the rain — got a fire going — come in and dry off a bit," said Ghislain in his deep, raspy voice. Ghislain was a large and sturdy man. If Auren was the strongest twelve-year-old that

Ethan had ever seen, Ghislain was his adult equivalent, being one of the strongest men Ethan had ever met.

Ethan was shivering from the brisk morning and was glad to be out of the rain. The fireplace was a sight to be seen, with stone that reached from floor to ceiling. It almost took up the entire wall, and had a distinctly large opening. The fire crackled with charred logs that had broken in half and nestled in the warm glow from hours of burning. It instantly warmed Ethan as he held his hands toward the fire.

Ghislain's wife, Isabel, was in the kitchen preparing breakfast for the boys. She was very strict with Auren. Before Isaac went missing, he and Ethan would frequently get scolded for their pranks by Auren's mother. Even Ghislain, with his enormous build, would tremble at the slightest hint of Isabel's wrath. But since the disappearance of Isaac, Isabel was much more compassionate with Ethan. She always welcomed him with home-cooked meals and ensured he was keeping up with his studies.

Isabel brought out food and set it on the table in the great room. Fried eggs, tomatoes, sausage, biscuits, and a pudding were served, as well as a large pot of hot honeyed tea. Ethan especially enjoyed Mrs. Faryndon's food. A full meal was rare for him, growing up without a woman in the house.

"Thanks, Mrs. Faryndon, it's great," said Ethan through a mouth stuffed full of food.

"Yes, my dear Isabel, thank you. It's wonderful," added Odin, not daring to speak with a full mouth in fear of getting scolded.

"No problem, boys, just be sure you finish everything I put out here for ya. You'll be needin' your energy," she said politely.

She was setting out more biscuits and Ethan noticed something he had not seen until now. Isabel had a funny-looking scar on her wrist. Ethan thought it looked similar to a spider's web, except with a larger pattern. Isabel noticed Ethan looking at her arm and pushed her sleeves down as she headed for the kitchen. Ethan turned and stared at the fire in hopes that he had not offended her in any way.

"So Ethan, Auren tells me that you two encountered a werewolf last night?" asked Ghislain.

"Uh, yeah," stuttered Ethan

"Boy that must have been exciting, I haven't seen one of them in almost twenty years! Yes, that must have been exiting indeed," said Ghislain, chuckling.

"So you didn't see the werewolf?" asked Ethan.

Ghislain looked a bit surprised. "Well I can say most definitely not, I woulda known if I ran into a beast like that."

"Well how did Odin—" But Ethan was quickly cut off.

"He may not look it, but I suppose Odin has been known to handle himself quite well in a given situation," he said in his deep voice as he smiled at Odin.

"I barely made it out with my skin attached," laughed Odin. "Like the time you got stuck to the Lake Hunter's tongue — or when you found the magic healing herbs!" Odin and Ghislain laughed loudly.

"Oh, I almost forgot about those! I got so sick — bet I turned three shades of green!" Ghislain was laughing so hard that his eyes were tearing up a bit.

Ethan was starting to realize that these two had quite a history together. They were like two old chums that had been parted for a while. Auren, bored, was now slumped over with his chin resting on his hand. Ethan thought the old stories were fascinating, as he had never heard of this side of his old caretaker.

"Well then," said Odin. "Down to business, how would you two like to run an errand for Ghislain and me?"

Auren's head perked up and he sat at attention.

"What sort of errand?" asked Ethan, curious.

Odin reached into his pack, pulled out a large metal shackle and placed it on the table with a clank. It had two spikes that protruded from the inside of the ring and a locking mechanism on the outside. It was made of iron and showed signs of rust, or possibly blood that had dried and crusted along the inner edge.

"What is it?" asked Auren.

"It is a means of control for an uncontrollable beast," said Ghislain.

"You mean the werewolf?" asked Ethan.

"Actually, Wegnel said it's a Stonewolf," replied Auren smugly.

"Correct...," answered Odin, "...on both accounts. The creature is known as the Stonewolf for obvious alterations made to its skin. And *this* device, which was until recently attached, is called a pinch-shackle. They have been around for years and years — very old alchemy associated with devices such as these."

Ethan sat forward in his chair. "What do you mean?"

"What I mean to say is someone, or some*thing*, was attempting to control this creature. What I don't know is who, or what." Odin grabbed a small pair of glasses from his pack and held them out in front of his face to further examine the device. "I have never seen one quite this size before — notice the markings where the shackle pinches shut — some type of pattern there."

Ghislain leaned in. "Looks like a large chain connects to it ... yet — there doesn't appear to be any real damage to the contraption."

"Exactly," murmured Odin. "Which can only mean one thing."

"Yep," chuckled Ghislain.

"Well … what?" exclaimed Auren.

"The creature didn't escape … it was set loose," answered Ethan, looking both disturbed and excited that he had come to the proper conclusion.

"Correct," said Odin.

The boys looked at each other and then back at Odin, who was still examining the device through his glasses.

"How exactly did you say you got this off the Stonewolf?" asked Ghislain.

"I didn't say," quipped Odin, lifting his chin to remind Ghislain of the giant gashes the Stonewolf had left on his face. "Let's just say it was at my own personal expense…."

Ghislain nodded.

"When you said alchemy was a part of this, what exactly did you mean?" asked Ethan.

"What I mean is, certain metal objects can have alchemical properties associated with them. This particular object, made of iron, has elements of manipulation outside the standard forging process," explained Odin.

"You sounded like Wegnel for a second there," chuckled Auren.

"Indeed," replied Odin as he put the glasses back in his pack, pulling out a piece of scrap parchment. "Although I am hesitant to say, it may be more alarming that the creature itself was still alive, having been altered through alchemical manipulation. No doubt the last werewolf that Ghislain saw, several years ago, is the very same Stonewolf that was seen here in Strahlung," he added, making a rub of the markings on the pinch-shackle with the scrap of parchment. Odin held the rub and looked at it through the light of the fireplace. Satisfied with his work, he rolled the parchment up and placed it in his pocket.

"This leads us to your errand, boys," said Ghislain, fidgeting with the pinch-shackle. "Seems I used to make runs to Tirguard now and again, however I'm afraid that I must stick around home or get into trouble with Mrs. Faryndon …," Ghislain ended in a whisper, "and Odin here could no longer fight his way out of a paper bag, if you — er, know what I mean." He chuckled at Odin. "I need you two to investigate this symbol in Tirguard and bring back—"

But Ghislain was interrupted by Ethan. "Did you say Tirguard?" Ghislain slumped back in his chair and remained silent. Ethan then looked over to Odin. "Well, let's have it then — this place is real? Tirguard, it exists?" asked Ethan loudly.

"It does," answered Odin.

"How long have you known? All of you! HOW LONG?"

The room stayed silent for a few moments and then Odin took a deep breath. "I have known all along, Ethan," replied Odin. The deep gashes in his withered face brought little sympathy from Ethan.

"My brother has been missing for over three years. I have missed school … and missed out on so many other things to go and look for him, and it turns out there is a secret city that everyone knows about but me? How is this possible?"

"Ethan, you have every right to be angry, but please listen for a moment." Gesturing for Ethan to calm down, Odin leaned forward. Flecks of light from the fireplace reflected off his weathered eyes. "Long ago, there was a Curse placed on you … placed on all of us. Anyone that gave information about the Oroborus, or even spoke the creature's name, would reap the wrath of the Curse of Silence. As of the last few months, the Curse seems to be lifting…."

Ghislain lifted both hands up and motioned for Odin to stop speaking.

"What wrath?" asked Ethan sharply.

"NO! That's enough talk of that, Odin, my wife is here — my son!" exclaimed Ghislain in a whisper.

"Ghislain, I will only speak of what is known to be safe, I promise." He turned to Ethan and continued. "Please no questions, Ethan — for now — there are still things to confirm. However … there are three things I can tell you. First, travel by Oroborus to and from Tirguard is limited to a select few families. Second, people have been speaking of the Oroborus and not suffering penalty — more and more people are traveling by Oroborus again. And finally, breaking the Curse of Silence means instant death for anyone that does so. Which means, if something is spoken that is still forbidden by the Curse, everyone in this room could be in mortal danger."

Ethan did not know what to say; he sat back in his chair and kept silent. Ghislain had stopped fidgeting with the pinch-shackle and had quite a nervous look on his face. Auren was eager to break the silence. "So are we goin' then? I mean, is it safe? Won't everyone be talking about the Oroborus?"

"Now that we know Wegnel sent Ethan there successfully, we think it's assumable that you will be safe," answered Odin.

"Wegnel's services haven't been used regularly in years. Most folks just go about their business — some even completely unaware such travel exists," added Ghislain as he looked over his shoulder to see if Isabel was listening.

"We'll go," said Ethan abruptly.

Odin seemed pleased, and even Ethan was happy about the new possibilities unfolding in front of him. Ethan realized this plan was premeditated, for some of the items that Odin had packed seemed odd for simply going to Ghislain's house. Perhaps Ghislain and Odin wanted the boys to investigate a Stonewolf, but a much different task was on Ethan's agenda. He decided he and Auren could explore the map, and maybe they would get clues to help them find Isaac.

Odin, Ghislain, and the two boys grabbed their things and started on their way to Wegnel's hut. The short journey was quite cheerful. The rain had died down and the sun was peeking through the dreary morning sky. Odin and Ghislain went on about the past and how they were on many misbehaved adventures, which seemed to steadily bore Auren. Ethan, on the other hand, had never heard about this side of Odin or Ghislain. He had always thought that Odin's idea of excitement was sitting in the study drinking tea in front of the fire. They arrived at Wegnel's place, where they found Wegnel waiting for them outside.

"Well hello there," said Wegnel, scratching his beady-eyed wrinkly face. "It's great of you to show up on time for a change — not saying that you are the regular sort by any means, but you—"

"That's quite enough pleasantries, Wegnel, we don't have time for all the babble this trip." grumbled Ghislain.

The brash comment was overlooked by the alchemist and he continued. "Ah then, come inside," said Wegnel quickly.

Ghislain and Auren walked in first, followed by Odin, and then Ethan made his way up the stairs and into the hut. It seemed much more cramped with Ghislain and Odin inside. Ethan looked at the chair in which his first meeting with the Oroborus had taken place. It looked rather unique, but at the same time, quite plain. It was made of wood but had a dark border around the backrest and seat. Everyone found a place to sit except for Ethan and Wegnel. Ethan did not care to sit in that chair, not now anyways. He stood by the doorway and watched Wegnel as he rooted around the kitchen.

"Any tea?" yelled Wegnel from the other room.

"No, thank you," replied Odin.

Ghislain looked annoyed. "Let's get down to business already, Wegnel."

Wegnel came in the room with a familiar small bottle of red powder.

"Oh, no — no son of mine will have need for any blundering blinding powder — not today or any day," said Ghislain sternly.

Wegnel looked a bit disappointed but put down the red powder and instead approached the beautiful chest with metal workings on the front, opened it, took out the silk bag and placed it on the table. Wegnel loosened the drawstring and took the creature from the bag. Auren's mouth was agape as he stared at the Oroborus.

"Ethan, why don't you sit down first, since you have done this already," said Odin.

Ethan picked up the pack that Odin had brought and had a seat in the old wooden chair. Wegnel placed the leather straps around his arms and turned to get the Oroborus.

"Now then, it will be important to remember not to panic, for when you arrive on the other side you will have to wait quite some time for Auren to show. It could be several minutes it could, and you don't want to be getting yourself all irate."

The Oroborus had removed its tail from its mouth. The colors had altered slightly, as well as the shape. The tail was bright blue on the bottom, had brilliant yellow lines running up to the top, all surrounded by a black border.

"His tail looks different than the last time I saw it," said Ethan, wondering if he should panic.

"Ah yes, that has much to do with little, and little to do with many things. You see, he has never had to necessitate for feelings, but as time passes and he spends more time around humans, he finds himself wanting to express himself, wanting to express his … feelings. I believe this is a display of contentment for his environment I do. Evidently, Dimon has somehow come to the conclusion that you are of quality folk, how he came to that I may never know, but there you have it," rambled Wegnel.

As Wegnel brought the Oroborus closer to Ethan's forearm, Odin noticed something. Dimon's eyelids had slowly peeled open to reveal two very large black eyes. Odin looked up at Ghislain, who was also alerted by the eyes that had just appeared. Ghislain was just about to speak when the Oroborus opened its mouth and sank its teeth into Ethan's forearm. Ethan needed no reminder of what it felt like, and slipped away into darkness.

Auren's Bucket

Ethan awoke disoriented; his hands were clenching the arms of the magic chair as if to catch himself from falling. He opened his eyes to a blurry mug of wrinkles and two beady eyes staring down at him. It was MacArthur.

"Ahhh yes, I knew I would see you again, my boy," said MacArthur. "So you believe in Tirguard now?"

"Yeah, but—"

"I assume you are bringing company this time around?"

"Yeah … but how did you…?" Ethan asked, his eyesight clearing up.

"They come by themselves and then they bring others, I have seen it a thousand times over. Besides, it's my business to know these kinds of things," said MacArthur. "Please, rest over here." He pointed to the comfy chair. Ethan made his way over and plopped down in the cozy seat. MacArthur was carrying a mug of tea in one hand and a bucket in the other; he brought the tea over to Ethan and set it on the end table.

"Thanks," said Ethan, in anticipation of watching the magical chair in action for the first time. MacArthur nodded and took a seat himself, placing the bucket to the side on the floor, both now staring at the chair.

"What does it look like … you know, when someone comes through?" asked Ethan.

"Hard to explain really — it's best if one sees it for themselves."

Ethan leaned back to peer out the window. "Is it early morning here?"

"Indeed, the sun should be coming up any moment now."

"But how—" stuttered Ethan.

"Time difference," answered MacArthur shortly, with his eyes fixated on the chair.

Ethan remembered MacArthur describing a time difference but was still unclear as to what he meant. From his dealings with Wegnel, he thought it may be better not to pry. Ethan was much more eager to see what it would look like when Auren arrived. As he continued to stare at the chair in front of him, he noticed it was identical to the chair in Wegnel's hut.

MacArthur had a peek at the pack that Ethan carried with him. "Staying a while then?" he inferred.

Ethan also looked down at his pack that had been prepared by Odin. "Yes," he answered awkwardly. He did not know if it was the right time to reveal his true plans to MacArthur. Maybe it was best to wait for Auren to arrive before discussing anything.

At that very moment the border around the chair started to glow softly. It was getting stronger, growing in brightness until it hurt Ethan's eyes. Then a flash erupted from the chair. Ethan could not bear it and had to shield his eyes. Suddenly it stopped. Ethan looked up to find a figure sitting in the chair; it was much smaller than he had expected, and appeared to be female.

"Availia?"

"How do you know the Oroborus didn't turn Auren into a girl?" asked Availia, smiling.

"How did — er, what are you doin' here?" stuttered Ethan.

Availia stood on her toes and gave Ethan a quick hug. "I arrived at Wegnel's right after you left, and Auren was kind enough to let ladies go first. Besides, he thought it would be funny if you were expecting him instead of me."

"But what are you doing here?"

"Well, I *was* trying to win the youth sword competition so I could be squad leader in the Guard. But as you, Auren, and no doubt everyone else saw, I lost to stupid Marcus Grenwise — the miscreant of Whitehaven. I need to thank Auren for paddling his bottom and making him look like an idiot — you two are hilarious, remember the toads?" asked Availia, smiling.

"But what about the Curse? How do you even know this place

exists?" asked Ethan curiously.

"Oh, the Curse of Silence? That's over with. Besides, my family is exempt — we trade goods with Tirguard all the time. My parents wouldn't let us talk about it outside the house, you know … with the threat of death and the Curse and all that. My sister is in the Guard here as well. But this is my first time in Tirguard — so exciting!" exclaimed Availia.

Ethan scratched his head for a moment as he took everything in. Just then another blinding flash of light ignited the room.

"Oh, that was an odd trip," groaned Auren. "I thought I might lose my breakfast for a…." His face turned green, then pale, and then green again. MacArthur was ready for this, for he immediately handed him the bucket, and Auren ended up losing his breakfast *three times.* He lifted his sweaty face out of the bucket, looked around, and looked back to MacArthur. "You look just like Wegnel," he panted.

"Well, my dear boy, that's because I *am* Wegnel."

"Right then," he answered with his head drooping back in the bucket.

"Your father had a weak stomach too, you probably best not mention it to his face though," suggested MacArthur.

"So are you two here to enroll?" interrupted Availia.

"Enroll in the Guard? Uh … no, we are here to investigate an attack," answered Ethan.

"Stonewolf," echoed Auren's voice out of the bucket.

"Did he say *Stonewolf?*" asked Availia, tilting her head to the side.

"Indeed he did," replied MacArthur. "And if I am not mistaken, it is referred to by alchemical experts as a stone lycanthrope, or … *Stonewolf.* Altering a man to become a wolf, and then a second alteration takes place, inducing a stone-fleshed exterior — simply an amazing creature."

"And," Ethan pulled the pinch-shackle out of his pack, "we have this." He handed the device to MacArthur.

"A pinch-shackle — are you sure? It would be nearly impossible to control a creature that powerful with a childish device like this. Although the size … *seems* accurate," MacArthur mused while studying the device.

"Well, yeah. I saw it on the Stonewolf's leg, but at the time I didn't know what I was looking at. So you're saying it wouldn't work?" asked Ethan.

"Not likely," said MacArthur. He turned the shackle around and noticed the small symbol in the metal. "Did you see this marking?"

Ethan nodded.

"Well … it doesn't look familiar to me — but one would use some type of symbol to initiate control of the wearer of a pinch-shackle. As I said, I don't know how this could work — there is no possible way one man could control a creature such as this … I mean, if there were, he would have to be a master alchemist … and even then … not likely." MacArthur handed the pinch-shackle back to Ethan. "Sorry I can't be of more help. You two must have made quite an impression on someone — being placed in charge of such a daunting task."

Auren raised his head from the bucket, looked over to Availia and Ethan, and then to MacArther. "Well, Father said Ethan made an impression on the Oroborus — does that count?"

"What do you mean?" asked Ethan with his eyebrows raised.

"Dimon opened his eyes," said Availia. "It's supposedly a trait of the Oroborus, that it doesn't need to see — so it never opens its eyes, but it did just before you passed through."

"She speaks the truth, Ethan," said MacArthur. "In fact, Dimon had not even developed eyelids until about five hundred years ago. He has never opened them before, until…," MacArthur paused, scratching his balding head, "actually, on your last trip from here I noticed that the Oroborus looked at you."

Ethan was confused and was about to ask why this was a big deal.

MacArthur continued. "This is truly a significant event, and it is so because he has opened his eyes only one other time." Ethan looked startled. "He opened them … to look at your brother," said MacArthur, now in a very serious voice.

"*Isaac?*" exclaimed Ethan, "but why?"

"I am not sure I am the best one to answer that. And for that matter, I am not entirely certain. Dimon is very particular about who he inflates his curiosity upon. It may be that he senses in you the same quality that he sensed in Isaac," replied MacArthur.

At this point Auren felt like he was in the general store and Vincent was talking Ethan up again. But it did not matter to Auren; still feeling sick, he threw up in the bucket again, paused, and looked back up to MacArthur. "Do you know where we can find Isaac then?" Auren asked weakly. Ethan looked at the alchemist as if he had asked the question himself.

"Ah…," MacArthur paused. "I see … unfortunately, I do not know his current whereabouts."

"Do you know where we could start looking then?" asked Ethan desperately. "Just anything that could give us a clue … anything?"

"Well, you could try the records department. They keep records of all important activity in Tirguard. It may even give you answers about the Stonewolf attack you're investigating, but there is no way to get near there, unless of course…."

"Unless what, MacArthur?"

"Well, unless you were enrolled in the Guard — civilians are not allowed near the records department," answered MacArthur.

"Looks like you two will be going to orientation with me after all," exclaimed Availia.

"Oh, man," grumbled Auren. He had regained the color in his cheeks and was starting to feel relief from the effects of Oroborus travel. He looked out the window and smiled. "Hey, is it morning again? Looks like I get another chance at eating breakfast!"

Ethan and Availia shook their heads.

Orientation

The three stepped out of the hut and into a bustling city. Ethan remembered the market district and recognized the vendor carts, colorful banners and the smell of food wafting past. He knew the smells would certainly excite Auren's appetite and it would only be a matter of time before they bought food from one of the vendors. Auren started toward a meat pie shop, but at that very moment he stopped in his tracks.

"That rat-faced *jerk* is here," hissed Auren.

Both Ethan and Availia looked where Auren was pointing. "Just wait a minute, Auren. Maybe he doesn't want to start any trouble, and it's probly best if we—"

"Like heck he's not! He's already picking on that boy,"

interrupted Availia. She immediately started walking toward Marcus Grenwise and his entourage.

"Well, mate, we can't let her go by herself, can we?" asked Auren, smiling.

"Um … okay," Ethan hesitantly agreed. "Let's go make friends again."

A very pale boy was standing with his eyes aimed at his feet. He was wearing all black and had an expressionless face. Marcus and his followers were taunting the boy, but did not seem to get any type of reaction.

"What's the matter, stuttering Stanley? Cat got your tongue? …or maybe I should get my wardog to use you as a chew toy."

"Mm … mm … mustn't mingle — many miscreants mm … m … morons," stuttered Stanley.

"What?!" yelled Marcus as he drew his sword.

"You heard him, you moron! Why don't pick on someone your own size," challenged Ethan, now standing between Stanley and Marcus.

Marcus turned as if to walk away and then lunged his sword right past Ethan and into Stanley's shoulder. Ethan jumped and took a step back toward his friends, but to his surprise, Stanley did not move an inch.

"WHAT DID YOU DO THAT FOR?" yelled Auren, both him and Availia looking shocked.

"If they have a prison here, I guarantee you'll be in it soon!" yelled Ethan as he grimaced at the sight of a sword sticking into flesh.

He took a step forward to countermand Marcus, but was stopped short. Marcus quickly removed his sword from Stanley's shoulder and held it up to Ethan's throat.

"There is no law against stabbing a dead person — ol' stuttering Stanley will be my personal pincushion while I'm here," taunted Marcus. He drove the sword forward until it depressed Ethan's skin.

"Stanley's shirt," said Stanley, placing his finger through the hole in his shirt as he inspected it.

"*Dead?*" asked Ethan as he stood his ground. "What do you mean *dead?*"

"WHAT IS GOING ON OVER THERE?" yelled a familiar voice. Ethan would recognize the over-dressed man anywhere. It was Tothyll.

Tothyll had selected a classy brown coat accompanied by an open-collared shirt and an assortment of jewelry. His shoes were so shiny that Ethan could see his reflection in them. He had a ring on almost every finger and on his thumbs as well.

"You make me sick, Marcus!" yelled Tothyll as he grabbed Marcus' collar with both hands and pulled him face to face. "If I see you act out again, I will not hesitate — you understand?"

Marcus nodded.

"Now scram! I don't need any trouble the first day of orientation."

Marcus withdrew his sword from Ethan's neck and sheathed the thin double-edged blade.

"Watch your back, Ethan," smirked Marcus under his breath.

"He doesn't have to as long as we're around," replied Auren. Availia crossed her arms and nodded as the gang of miscreants walked away laughing.

Ethan caught his breath and shook the hand of his savior.

"Thanks, Tothyll," said Ethan.

"No problem — nothing you wouldn't have handled anyway. You alright, Stanley?" asked Tothyll, now investigating the hole in Stanley's shirt.

"Nn … nnn … yes," answered Stanley.

"That's a relief … Ethan, I would like you to meet Stanley — and Ethan, who are your friends here? A recruiter like myself has to know these things."

"This is Auren and Availia, but … wait — how is he okay? I saw a sword go right into his shoulder … I mean … I did, didn't I?"

"Alchemy accidents always anticipate anger and aggression," said Stanley quickly.

"Does he always talk like that?" asked Auren, pointing at Stanley.

"Stop it," snapped Availia, hitting Auren's arm. "You're being rude."

"On the contrary, it is only natural to be curious," replied Tothyll. "Stanley is a resident here. At one time he was a student in experimental alchemy — one of the school's finest. Several squads were attempting to make an elixir that could extend the life of an individual. After what seemed to be a successful attempt to keep an old cat from dying, Stanley tested it on himself. He is not entirely alive, but not quite dead either — more or less he is … well, stuck in a state of limbo between the two."

"Nnn … nn," stuttered Stanley.

"It's alright, Stanley, I will get to that," Tothyll continued. "The trauma associated with the experiment left him without proper speech. However, he has worked with a specialist and now he is able to communicate. I believe you are returning to school this year, aren't you, Stanley?"

"Nnn … nn … yes," answered Stanley, while playing with the hole in his shirt again.

"Stanley," said Availia, as she approached. "Did this hurt?"

"Stanley's shirt," replied Stanley.

Availia inspected the hole in Stanley's shirt and then looked at the skin where the sword would have gone through. "There's no wound here — it's as if nothing happened at all. But something did happen. Stanley, those boys were very rude, do you understand?"

Stanley nodded.

"So, uh … what happened to the cat?" asked Auren, chuckling.

"I'm sorry?" asked Tothyll, scratching his head.

"You know — that was treated with experimental alchemy — before Stanley tried it on himself."

"Yes … well, I … you know, I am not entirely sure. That's a good question, Auren, I would be happy to look into it for you." Tothyll gave the four a rather strange look and then refocused. "Ethan, I know last time we spoke you didn't seem interested in the Guard, but here you are on the first day of orientation. There is still time to enter your name in the Ordo Electus lottery … well … I …

can enter all of your names if you like."

"What lottery?" asked Ethan.

"Well, this year is different, as it is the first open enrollment in some time. But in the past, every teacher was assigned a squad of four at random. However, I am afraid to say that there are concerns with several teachers on the quality of, well … shall we say, talent … that comes through the Oroborus. So it was decided that this year's lottery be a selection instead. After today's orientation is concluded, all twenty-five teachers will take turns selecting one member of their squad per round for a total of four rounds, until they have four students, which means only one hundred students will make the cut this year. And the results will be posted outside the orientation building upon completion — how exciting!"

"Whoa, that sounds wicked! Can we watch?" asked Auren.

"Sorry — closed door event," answered Tothyll. "If you would have me, I could still get your names entered into the Electus — you in then?"

Ethan looked at Auren, who shrugged his shoulders but nodded slightly. They both turned to Availia as she smiled and nodded.

"I would also add that if I sign you up and you are selected … well … let's just say that is how I make a living," added Tothyll.

"We're in," answered Ethan.

Tothyll again shook Ethan's hand and smiled. "Well then, Stanley, could you show these three to orientation? I am sure they are excited to get started."

Stanley nodded.

"Orientation?" asked Ethan. "But don't we need to be selected first?"

"Orientation is for anyone that is new to the city of Tirguard — the first class is mandatory, I'm afraid … and starts in a few minutes — other classes are mandatory if you wish to leave the walls of Tirguard. The class will be filled with those from Whitehaven that are trying to join the Guard — should be fun … right?"

Availia nodded and took Stanley by the arm. Ethan and Auren followed as they were led through the city to a rather boring-looking building. Ethan, who felt they were making very little progress with getting answers, reluctantly approached the old wooden door at the main entrance. A small sign hung over the door that read '*Orientation*'.

"Nnnn … nnn … good, nnggg … nnn … luck," stuttered Stanley.

"Thanks, Stanley! We will see you again, maybe you can show us around later," said Availia.

"Nnnnggg … nnn … sure," replied Stanley, withholding a small smile.

The trio pushed through the swinging door. The hinges squeaked as they hissed open and the three found themselves in a large classroom which was dreary and dismal. It had several seats, cracked wooden desks with splinters sticking out, and old yellowed parchment supplied at each desk. The others in the class appeared to have been there all morning. Some of them had curled up in a corner and were resting their eyes, while others were looking at books and old scrolls that they had brought. Ethan noticed one boy carrying a decent-sized armor bag that had armor hanging out the side. It was obvious to Ethan that the boy had intentions of using it. Looking around the room, Ethan realized that he, Auren, and Availia were of the few that did *not* have an armor bag with them.

"And what do you think you're doing here?" shrilled a voice from the other side of the room.

Ethan recognized the voice immediately; it was Marcus Grenwise.

"You planning on registering for the Guard? It's really no matter anyhow, you and your stupid friends won't make the top one hundred," added Marcus.

"We don't really care about the Guard, you moron," spouted Auren without thinking. He realized that all the children in the room that were carrying armor bags intended to join the Guard. But it was too late; soon they were receiving dirty looks from around the room.

"Then why are you here?" asked Marcus. The question went unanswered. "I see you're still a stupid oaf — soon you'll learn how to talk to your superiors with respect," snapped Marcus.

"And who exactly would that be?" asked Ethan.

"Me! In case the rules of the youth sword competition fell on deaf ears. Winner of the contest becomes captain of the youth Guard. That's why so many entered — didn't really matter though … just more for me to defeat," answered Marcus snidely.

Ethan looked over to Auren, who had entered the competition. "That true?" he whispered.

"Well yeah, I guess — wasn't really paying attention to that part of it, wasn't concerned with the prize at the time," whispered Auren.

Ethan nodded and refocused on Marcus, who was still staring at them with cold eyes. "Well you don't have to worry about us being in your youth Guard, Marcus. If *you're* running it, I would rather jump off a cliff," said Ethan.

"Not even you, Availia?" asked Marcus. "I was certain when I saw your application to the tournament that you had expressed a high interest in the Guard, but if not, I will be sure to pass that information along so none of you get in."

Availia's hands formed two fists and her face turned bright red. Ethan could not tell if she was going to cry or rip Marcus' head off.

"Tell me, Ethan, how does it feel to have a big stupid oaf as a best friend?" spat Marcus.

Auren had just sat down, but bolted out of his chair as if he wanted to punch Marcus. Ethan put his hand on Auren's shoulder and pushed him back in his seat.

"Dunno, how does it feel to almost get taken out of the youth sword competition by a girl who has more talent in her right hand than you have in your entire body?" spouted Ethan.

"Or maybe you want to talk about how a big stupid oaf spanked you in the backside in front of hundreds of people," snickered Auren.

"Or how you pick on, draw your sword, and attack an unarmed boy," added Availia.

"I'd be surprised if they put you in charge of washing dishes, let alone other people," added Ethan.

Marcus' cheeks started to turn red. "At least I wasn't scared to enter the contest because of my poor brother — ahh, boo-hoo," he mocked.

Just then, the door of the shabby classroom opened fiercely, interrupting the debate. In stepped a shady-looking but well-dressed man. He was led by his slightly large nose, which he carried in front of him with abrupt authority. He walked to the front of the classroom without worrying about the door, which reached the end of its hinges and snapped back. Alerted, all of the students sat up and came out of their daze.

The man placed some fresh scrolls on the desk in front, and with a stern look walked right down the middle of the room to the back of the class. He then peered around at everyone.

"Sit … down," ordered the man. Everyone who was standing sat down, including Ethan.

"I see all of the civilized families must have run out of noble sons to send forthwith," he said in a very precise and sharp voice. He leaned over and looked down at Ethan. "And some would not even have the courtesy to send decent armor…," he said quietly as he made his way to the front of the classroom at a slow, intimidating pace, "…or in some cases, provide any at all." Some of the others looked over at the three, who gave each other a look and then kept their heads down. "I am Captain of the armies of Tirguard. My name is Heinrich Cornelius Agrippa, but of course, you will refer to me as *Captain* Heinrich Agrippa. This is one of many classes you *must* take before leaving the walls of Tirguard … so pay attention. I am not here out of free will, so do not waste my time with silly questions or stories of why … *you* … are here, because … I do not care," he said with his hands behind his back. His eyes rolled over everyone in the classroom, who were now paying much closer attention.

He paused for a bit and then continued. "It seems to me that some of you may think you can come and go as you please. Allow me to inform you otherwise — there is only one word here — my word. There is only one law here, and that is the law of Tirguard — which is the law you will follow during your stay here." He paused again and paced slowly to the front corner of the classroom. "You see, some of you … who arrived through MacArthur, may think you can travel unchecked. However, I am here to inform you that he has been detained … and you will now only move back and forth through me, by appointment. No exceptions!" he shrilled.

Auren and Ethan glanced at each other while whispering broke out within the classroom, which was immediately interrupted.

"If … you have a concern with this, I will be most happy to escort you down to the prison, where you may tell your woes and sorrows to a cellmate … of your choosing." The class quieted down. "No questions? Good, I will move along then," he said smugly. "There are a few things to keep in mind. For those of you who wish to spend any amount of time in Tirguard, know that thirty years here is equivalent to one year in Enterom. For those of you who remain uneducated…," he peered over at Auren, "Enterom is where you came from, the other side of the Oroborus, so to speak," he smiled, curling his lip.

Ethan grew more uncomfortable as Heinrich continued his

lesson. "Some of you have interest in joining the Guard. Trust me when I say that the reward is great. If you excel in the Guard, you will have an opportunity to join with one of the armies of Tirguard. And, if lucky, could serve directly under myself … here," continued Heinrich. "We have the most imperative job … here, in the army of Tirguard. We protect the city from the Mitan race. They are a murderous group. Outside the city walls, they have destroyed, pillaged, and hunted animal, beast, and man. For those of you that think travel is easy, let me inform you that you will not find horses in Tirguard — all are dead. Hunted down and killed by the Mitans. When they ran out of animals and beasts to hunt, they started hunting men. If you do find a creature in the wild, be wary, because it was most likely too difficult for a Mitan hunter to kill." Heinrich peered around the classroom to look for a reaction.

"Now then, write your name, your family's surname, and the town in which you reside on the parchment in front of you — indicate if you have interest in the Guard. After completion, take a copy of our laws which you will … abide by, and be on your way. Any questions? No? Good." Heinrich turned on a heel, opened the door, and walked out.

"Well then," said Auren. "That was fun. He seemed tightly wound to me, did he seem tightly wound to you?"

"Yeah — but what about MacArthur?" asked Ethan.

The boy with the decent-sized armor bag looked over at Ethan. "You lot are a distraction. Do yourselves a favor … leave." He got up and placed his finished parchment on the front desk, took a copy of the laws, hurled his armor bag over his shoulder and walked out the door.

"Well then, we just made another friend," said Auren quietly.

"You won't last one day here," threatened Marcus as he placed his parchment on the desk and headed through the door.

Ethan looked over to Availia. "Sorry about that. I hope we didn't ruin your chances of getting in the Guard."

"Well, my sister is one of the highest-ranking squad captains here, so I think I may still have a chance. But maybe it's best to keep to ourselves for now, just in case," said Availia, who was secretly disappointed.

Ethan and Auren agreed; they brought their parchment to the front and each took a copy of the laws before making their way out the door. Heinrich was waiting just outside for them.

"Can't believe we have to take more classes from this buffoon before leaving the city," whispered Auren.

"Considering he put MacArthur in prison, now we don't have any way of getting back — well, don't think we have any choice really," muttered Ethan.

"Not unless we make an appointment with Heinrich," corrected Availia. "Although, I don't picture Heinrich as the type who would sit in a hut all day sending people back and forth."

"Hmm … well then, what do you think we should do about MacArthur?" asked Ethan.

"What *can* we do? I knew the old man was a bit crazy; it probably just caught up with him," replied Auren.

"He's not crazy … maybe a bit eccentric…."

"Ethan Wright, I presume?" interrupted Heinrich in a slimy voice. The three were caught off guard; Ethan wondered if Heinrich had heard their conversation. "I find it funny how features can carry one such as yourself through life," he continued as he placed his long white fingers under Ethan's chin and examined his face. Ethan noticed a silver ring with a large black stone on one of the fingers grasping his chin. The inside of the stone was swirling around like pluming black smoke, mesmerizing Ethan. He thought to himself that Heinrich had picked a ring that matched his personality and began to chuckle. The Tirguard Captain noticed Ethan's grin and pushed his face back. "You look just like your brother … the *traitor*."

"*What?* What did you say about my brother?"

Heinrich turned and strutted away, his hands behind his back as if he had not a care in the world. The boys looked at each other, confused. Availia put her hand on Ethan's shoulder.

"What do you think he meant by that?" asked Ethan, still upset over the comment.

"Not sure; but it sounds like he may know where your brother is," replied Availia.

"Yeah, but no way he's gonna say … it's pretty obvious he hates us," replied Auren.

"Hates *me* anyways," said Ethan.

"Don't look now, but here comes pasty again," said Auren, looking over his shoulder. Availia looked over and saw Stanley headed in their direction, and she promptly smacked Auren in the back of the head. "Ow, what was that for?!"

Availia looked upset. "His *name* is Stanley!" she said, appalled.

"All right, you don't have to hit me, ya lunatic, I just forgot his name is all!"

The pale boy wandered past and leaned against the adjacent building, looked down, and stared at his shoes. He started to play with the hole in his shirt.

"Hey there — Stanley!" called out Ethan. Stanley looked up at the three and smiled. "Do you have a few minutes to show us around then?"

In his haste, Stanley tripped over his own feet. "Yyy … yyy … ngh…." he stuttered, then finally nodded.

"Sounds good then," answered Auren. "Can you show us where to get some armor? We're the only idiots who didn't bring any."

"We aren't all idiots," stated Availia, smiling.

"What do you mean?"

"My sister has mine, I just have to go pick it up."

"You have armor?" asked Auren, jealous.

"Of course, I came here to join the Guard, didn't I?" shrilled Availia, getting ready to smack Auren in the shoulder this time. Auren put his hands up in submission.

"Okay, okay … sorry," he pleaded.

"Well, we may need armor too. Stanley, do you know where we can look for some armor?" asked Ethan.

Stanley nodded again and pointed back toward the market district. He smiled, and started in that direction. Ethan, Auren and

Availia paused for a moment.

"Looks like it's that way then," said Auren smartly. It was apparent by his pace that Stanley wasn't going to wait up, so the trio ran to catch up with him.

Ordo Electus

"Djinn!" screamed a voice. Stanley stopped in his tracks as a hooded figure pointed directly at the group. Auren walked right into the back of Stanley and stepped on the heels of his shoes. Stanley looked down and inspected his shoes, as if to ensure they were alright.

"You know, this is really getting annoying — you people calling him names!" yelled Auren, attracting passersby. Availia seemed impressed that Auren was standing up for Stanley.

"Djinn! Djinn!" yelled the figure, still pointing. The group could now see that the hooded figure was a wrinkled old woman. Her twisted face had a faded tattoo that encircled both eyes, which themselves were milky and disturbing to look at. Ethan would have thought her to be blind if she was not pointing right at them.

"I don't think she's talking to Stanley. I think she's … talking to you, Ethan," muttered Availia. Indeed, Stanley took a step to the side, and it became clear that the old hooded woman was pointing directly at Ethan.

"Me?" Ethan took several steps forward to study the old woman. Her teeth were rotten, her robe was filthy, and she had a particular odor of something spoiled. The smell was like one of Wegnel's experimental mystery pastes gone awry.

"I know … you speak for the dead," continued the woman.

Ethan examined the tattoo more closely. It looked decorative but very strange. "I don't speak for anybody," stated Ethan. "Do you recognize me?"

"Yes…."

"So you're talking about Ethan's twin brother then," interrupted Auren.

"No, him," answered the old woman, pointing at Ethan's face.

"You can buy armor over there," stated the old woman. Not breaking eye contact, she swung her pointed finger at a small building to Ethan's left. "But *you…*," she stuck her finger back at Ethan's forehead, "…won't need it — what you want is behind you." She turned and walked around a corner, toward the alleyway of the armor shop.

"Wait!" Ethan dashed around the corner, but the old woman had disappeared. "That was strange," he said to himself.

"What the heck is *djinn*, anyways?" asked Auren.

"Sssss, nnggh … spirit," answered Stanley. "Nnnggh, ngghh … dead," he added, playing with the hole in his shirt again.

"*Dead?*" whispered Ethan to himself. He stood in the walkway motionless. The thought of his brother being dead had crossed his mind, but he did not like to dwell on it.

"She looked a bit shallow in the eyesight department, maybe she was talkin' to you, Stanley," ventured Auren.

"No … at least, not unless Stanley has a twin brother too — think she meant me for sure," responded Ethan.

"Well, let's pick out some armor then, before it's all gone" said Auren, smiling while pointing at the armor shop.

The four looked up at the armor shop, only to see a sign in the window that read '*Sold Out*'.

"Sold out?" whined Auren as he stomped his feet.

"What you want is behind you," murmured Ethan.

"What?!" asked Auren.

"That's what the old woman said, 'what's behind you,'" answered Availia. "Look! There! We must've walked right past it." Availia was pointing at a small rickety cart in the middle of the road. There were small metal objects hanging from it, and an old man was leaning against the cart appearing to be half-asleep.

"Is that … a pinch-shackle?" inquired Ethan.

"They sell them on carts?!" chuckled Auren. "This place is great! Need to control some weird creature? You can sit and wait for a cart to drive by and — there you go!"

Ethan pulled the large pinch-shackle out of his pack and

dropped it on the small wooden table attached to the cart. It made a loud *clank* when it hit the surface, which startled the old man.

"What! What do you want? Scram!"

"Actually, we need to ask you a few questions about this device," announced Ethan.

"Questions?" grumbled the old man. "You gonna buy something?"

"Well, no…." started Ethan. The man gave Ethan a dirty look, but Availia intervened.

"I'm with Tanbe Trading — we only order in quantity, but before we place such a large order, we'll be checking with your competitors first," stated Availia smoothly.

"*Competitors?*" chuckled the old man. "I don't have any … *competitors* — so you'll be stuck with me, I'm afraid." He opened a drawer on his cart and pulled out a pair of spectacles. He wiped the lenses with his shirt and slid them on his face. "Let's take a look then." He lifted the pinch-shackle to his face and readjusted his glasses to examine the device more closely. Suddenly, he dropped it back on the table. "Where did you get this?" he demanded.

"Did you make it?" asked Ethan.

"I'll be asking the questions around here, sonny," groused the old man.

Auren could not hold his tongue. "Listen here, unless you want to be a part of an investigation started by the King himself, I suggest you start talking!"

"Now hold on just a second," placated the man. "Some bandit

had me make this bloody thing!"

"So you did make it?" pressed Availia.

"Yeah. This stranger wanted to control something rather large. He said it would be next to impossible, but promised me that if it worked he would pay a hefty price for it — haven't heard from him since."

"Who was this stranger?" asked Ethan.

"Not sure, never saw his face — he wore a cloak and only came 'round at night," answered the old man.

"So you custom-made and delivered one of these things to an unidentified man that promised to pay you … if it worked?" asked Auren disbelievingly.

"Don't judge me, boy. It was hard times back then — didn't sell anything for months … had to take a chance."

"Well then, tell us about this pinch-shackle. What kind of creature was the man going to use it for? What does this symbol mean?" insisted Availia.

"You already know what it was being used for, otherwise you wouldn't be here … werewolf," answered the man. "I told him it wouldn't be easy, it probly wouldn't work, unless—"

"Unless what?" asked Ethan.

"Unless he was an alchemist … a darn good one, too," he continued. "That symbol has certain alchemical properties. The trick is to use something else, like a ring or necklace, with the same symbol and alchemical properties. Then, *maybe*, you can get some type of control over a creature such as that — but still, not likely."

"So you made him some type of ring then?" asked Auren.

"Of course not! I gave him the recipe to make his own — not in the business of making jewelry. Besides … this way I'm not liable. I only sell the shackle — just the shackle. By itself, the thing may as well be a dog collar."

Ethan was getting tired. Stanley had taken them to nearly every armor shop in the city. Most were out of affordable armor, while others had inexpensive armor that simply would not fit. As evening descended, they approached the last armor shop in the city, only to find another sign on the front window stating it was '*Sold Out*'.

"With everyone trying to get into the Guard, we'll never find armor," sighed Auren. "You'd think we could find *something!* Used, dumpy old armor … *anything!*" Auren plopped down in front of the sold-out armor shop and slumped his head down. He ran his fingers through his hair and sighed again.

"You do know that we only need to be in the Guard to get access to the records department, right?" asked Ethan as he looked down at Auren.

"Well, yeah … of course I know that."

"It's just, you seem to be taking this a bit serious — don't ya think?"

Auren raised his head. "Well, maybe. Just wanna have another chance to best Marcus is all. He's such an idiot. But besides that, I'm excited to see what number I'll get picked … you know, in the lottery."

"Yeah, I do know. We won't need armor to find that out," answered Ethan.

"But you do need it for the first day of class," reminded Availia.

"It's not even that. Just the thought of getting my own armor, going to classes, learning how to fight — being a part of something, ya know? I don't think being in the Guard would be so bad — as long as Marcus wasn't there, that is." Auren stood up. "I bet I get picked in the top ten. A big guy like me, had a fair showing in the youth sword competition — I'm bound to get—"

"You were out in the third round," reminded Availia.

"Isn't that good?" argued Auren.

"Not really, no."

"But I lost to the winner."

"So did I."

"But I made it one round further than—"

This annoyed Ethan. "You guys, I don't think this is gonna get us closer to getting some armor, maybe if we—"

Just then a loud bell echoed throughout the city.

"What was that?"

"Nghhh nghhh ngh … the, nghhh … results," stuttered Stanley.

"*Results?*" asked Ethan. "Oh! The results of the Electus have been posted?"

Stanley nodded and motioned for them to follow. The four made their way through the market district and toward the orientation building. There were hundreds of would-be students standing on the cobblestone, surrounding a large board on the side of the building. Auren tried forcing his way through the crowd, but every time he pushed his way forward, someone would budge back in front of him. He started to make his way back to his friends when a small commotion broke out at the opposite side.

"Clear the way — now!" yelled Marcus. A small path opened, allowing him to approach the board. He walked through the crowd, bumping shoulders with anyone who was slightly in his way. He looked up at the board for a moment, turned, and smiled. "I was selected number one, by none other than Heinrich himself," said Marcus in a cocky voice. As he strode back through the crowd, he noticed the four waiting to get a look at the board.

"You won't see your names up there!" he taunted. "I had you removed from the Electus … all of you!"

Just then two figures emerged from the orientation building. The first one pushed the door so hard it nearly came off its hinges; it was Heinrich. The second figure Ethan did not recognize. He was an older man, a bit portly, and had small spectacles tucked in the front pocket of his white dress shirt. He was wearing a black jacket that hung nearly to the ground.

"Not exactly!" proclaimed the portly man as he approached Ethan and companions. "You must be Ethan Wright."

"Yeah," answered Ethan.

"My name is Edison Rupert. I will be your professor."

Heinrich forced his way through the crowd, bumping shoulders with Edison as he passed.

"Marcus! Grab the others and get to quarters, now!" spat Heinrich, in an obvious outrage. Marcus checked the board, grabbed the three other selections made by Heinrich and followed him down the street toward the spire.

"I am afraid things didn't exactly go according to Heinrich's plan," stated Edison, his wrinkled cheeks glowing from the chilled evening air. He leaned forward and shook hands with Ethan. "It is my absolute pleasure to finally meet you, Ethan."

"You too … what didn't go according to plan?"

"Oh, Heinrich withdrew your names from contention in the Electus," answered Edison. "I *was* number twenty-six, you see."

"Twenty-six!" yelled Auren. "That means I was selected twenty-sixth overall, that's … that's fantastic!"

Edison leaned over to Auren, whose face was now alight with admiration over the professor's last comment. "Auren Faryndon, is it? I, ahh … picked you second," revealed Edison.

"So … fifty-second?"

"No, my boy, twenty-seventh if you must know. I get the last choice in the first round, but the first choice in the second round, and so forth. But order was not important in this case." Edison grabbed the spectacles out of his front pocket and wiped the lenses. He placed them on his face so they straddled the tip of his nose, in order to get a better look at Ethan.

"So if Heinrich removed us from contention, how were you able to pick us at all?" inquired Ethan.

"And, I thought there were only twenty-five teachers in the Electus, not twenty-six," added Availia.

"Ah, yes. Availia, youngest sister in the Tanbe family. I felt absolutely thrilled to get you in the third round. If your name hadn't been removed from the list, you would have placed midway in the first round for certain!"

"Sir, how is it we got in the Guard?" asked Ethan again.

"My boy … you're not in the Guard. What a waste of talent that would have been!" exclaimed Edison, while pushing his spectacles all the way up his nose, removing them and then placing them back in his front pocket.

"What?" asked Ethan.

"I came out of retirement as the twenty-sixth member of the Electus to reopen the school of alchemy. You're going to be an alchemist."

"WHAT?" yelled Auren. "You mean, like *Wegnel?*"

"Well maybe not *that* good, we will see though, you know … no promises," answered Edison, smiling.

"So a retired alchemy professor is going to teach us … *what* exactly?" asked Availia. "I've trained with a sword for the past six years."

"Oh, swords are most useful, and it was more like an extended sabbatical than official retirement, it should be fun really, don't you think?"

"Yeah … fun," answered Auren, sighing again.

"Well, it will be for me anyhow. Let's see. I picked the twin brother of the most famous hero in the land, the son of Ghislain the mighty, and the younger sister to one of the best strategists and swordsmen … or should I say swords*women* that this city has ever seen!"

"But that's only three, don't the rules say that you need four?" asked Auren.

"You certainly know your stuff, Auren. I was particularly proud of my fourth selection; it took countless nights of research. I like to think of it as sort of a long shot. And it works out perfectly because he was in the school of alchemy before it closed down, he can't die, and he is standing right beside you — so I don't have to go looking for him … see … perfect!"

"Stanley?" asked Auren.

"I know, Auren, you may be thinking about the rules again, but I checked into it. Since he was put into this half-dead stasis, he technically hasn't aged a day, and therefore, isn't too old to join, it's simply perfect!" exclaimed Edison, clenching his hands together with a grin. "I think the only thing better than my four most perfect selections is Heinrich being angry about it!"

"And why would he get angry about it?" asked Ethan.

"Probably because he didn't get his way, or that you will not be under the jurisdiction of the Guard — who knows for sure," he answered as he motioned for his students to follow him. "Now then, it will get dark soon; we have to arrange for quarters. Since I just got here, and most everything was taken, we will have to settle for the school itself, at least for now."

As the five of them walked toward the school, Availia leaned in toward Auren. "At least you don't need to find armor now," she teased.

"Funny," replied Auren.

"So, where is the school anyways?" asked Ethan as they walked.

"Well, it is right up the street actually. Right around the corner up ahead … big stone building — oldest in the city, you can't miss it. Sort of an amazing story really. This building has withstood centuries of war, been under bombardment and even internal ridicule of practices contained within its doors. In fact, this school was one of the few buildings that existed before Tirguard itself existed … before mankind even discovered the Oroborus. It has withstood all of that, and here it is waiting for us to walk through its doors," he said as they approached a stone overhang affixed to the large building. Under the overhang there was a large door, also made of stone. Edison put his hand on the door, gave a slight push, and walked right through.

"*What?*" exclaimed Ethan.

"Where did he go?!" asked Auren.

"He just … walked *through* the door," stuttered Availia.

"Stanley soundly submits severing stone," said Stanley as he followed the professor through the door.

Ethan put his hand to the door and pushed, followed by Availia, and then Auren — but nothing happened. Auren continued to push on the door, trying to force it open, but it did not move.

"What just happened?" asked Ethan.

"Dunno," answered Auren.

Then Edison's head came through the door. "Did I mention that you have to be an alchemist to enter?" The large stone door swallowed Edison's chubby, wrinkled face. The remaining three looked as if they had seen a ghost as they continued to examine the door. Edison stepped through and startled all three again. This time he was carrying two sleeping bags, which he tossed on the ground. He reached through the door and pulled Stanley, who was also carrying two sleeping bags, back outside.

"Training starts tomorrow, you will all do it together as a team," announced Edison. "Night!"

"Ah … wait!" said Ethan. But it was too late; Edison had vanished through the door. Ethan turned to Stanley. "Stanley, how did *you* get through the door?"

"Ngghhh, ngghhh, sttt … Sanctuary … Stone Sanctuary," he answered.

"What's the Stone Sanctuary?" asked Availia.

"Ngghh ngghhh, difficult … nghhh ttttt, nghhhh … to … explain," he stuttered.

"It seems we have all night, Stanley," replied Ethan. The four unrolled their sleeping bags on the cold ground underneath the overhang of the old stone building. Ethan and Availia listened to Stanley's explanation as Auren grew bored and went to sleep. Not entirely satisfied with the information obtained, Ethan and Availia soon followed, as did Stanley.

On Sabbatical

"The Stone Sanctuary is where an alchemist of Tirguard is born. Just as you use your sword…," Edison looked over to Availia, "or your strength…," he peered at Auren, "your determination…," he placed his hand on Ethan's shoulder, "or your resourcefulness…," he nodded to Stanley, "you will use, combine, and protect yourself with all the options that alchemy has to offer. It will become a part of you, an extension of your body, infused in your mind, and course through the very fabric of your nerves," said Edison as he picked up a set of black jackets, much like his own, and handed them out. "And it all starts with these."

"Jackets?" asked Auren incredulously.

"Armor," corrected Edison.

Ethan examined the garment. It was coarse and hard in some areas, and less restrictive in others where movement might be a necessity. It had a particularly tall collar that he felt would cover his chin if buttoned all the way up. There were small metal fasteners that would clasp the front of the jacket closed. The back had a single thick grey bar that ran vertically down the center.

"This is armor?" asked Availia. "But my own armor is—"

"More restrictive? Heavy? Unable to conceal a weapon, tool of surprise, or method of escape?"

"Well yeah, but *this* can't take a direct hit from a sword," argued Availia.

"Then draw your sword, Availia, and we shall put your theory to practice," said Edison.

"But … isn't there another way to demonstrate?"

"Unfortunately not. And as your instructor, I realize I have not yet earned your respect or trust — now is as good a time as any." Edison fastened the top clasp of his alchemy jacket. The hardware sank down in the fabric, locking into place. The rest of the clasps fastened, one by one, down the length of the garment without the assistance of Edison. Each fastener was absorbed into the fabric, to look like small metal bars that held the front seam of the jacket together.

"Anything you see or learn here is between us or other students of alchemy under my instruction only," said Edison, placing both hands behind his back and putting weight on his front foot. "Now then, thrust your sword into my chest. Please take care to aim, as the collar *can* deflect upward strikes; however, I'm not wearing any protection on my face."

Auren stood with his mouth agape at the events unfolding. Availia handed her alchemy jacket to Ethan, leaned down, and pulled a sword out of her pack. She slowly unsheathed the thin double-edged blade.

"Are you sure?" asked Availia.

"Don't be afraid, you won't hurt me," reassured Edison.

Availia leaned forward and thrust the lightweight sword against the chest of their new instructor. Ethan stood in amazement as the garment reacted, pulling tight when struck, pushing the instructor back a few inches, but not piercing the jacket. The fabric seemed to contort to absorb the blow.

"What? How did …?" asked Ethan.

Edison touched the top clasp of his alchemy jacket and all of the fasteners opened. He pulled his spectacles from his front shirt pocket and examined them. "That was a very sturdy strike, Availia. I thought for a second that you may have damaged my favorite reading glasses, but they appear to be intact," said Edison, tucking the spectacles back into his front pocket.

"Whoa!" exclaimed Auren, unfolding his alchemy jacket and jamming his fists down the sleeves.

"Yes, yes, try them on. Get used to wearing them, as they were a great personal expense; I expect you will want to wear them often, and of course, every day in class."

The four put on their alchemy jackets. Auren clasped the top fastener on the collar and stuck his arms out to the side, waiting for the rest of the clasps to close on their own, but they did not. He peered downward to check the progress and lifted his head in anticipation for the miracle garment to close itself.

"Problem, Auren?" asked Edison.

"I think mine's broken — it's not doing the *thing*," he exclaimed.

"It's not? Defective, maybe?"

Ethan and Availia were having the same issue but, unlike Auren, were not making a production of it. Stanley's, on the other hand, fastened down as expected which left Auren frantically clasping and re-clasping the top fastener of his alchemy jacket.

"So, last night Stanley could get into the school. He walked right through the front door. And today, Stanley has control over his alchemy jacket — they fasten from top to bottom faster than you can wink an eye. So, what does Stanley have that you don't?" asked Edison as he paced back and forth in front of his students. Stanley held out his hand.

"Exactly!" exclaimed Edison, walking over to Stanley and examining his right hand. "Stanley bears the mark of the Stone Sanctuary. The mark of an alchemist — come and have a look. You see here, a curve upward and a curve downward, almost like the letter 'X', but not quite. This is the symbol for tin, which is viewed as the symbol of life, and also serves as a reminder that standing together is stronger than standing apart — as when you combine other elements with tin they immediately grow in strength."

"Does that mean that Stanley can control tin?" asked Availia, puzzled.

"Perhaps … but at the same time that is not the conclusion one should make," replied Edison. "That symbol means a lot of things, many of which reflect on strength, courage, and compassion. The alchemical secrets this symbol unlocks is part potential of the user and part mystery."

"What symbol do you have, professor?" asked Ethan.

"Ethan, my boy, we will get there, I promise … we will get there. But first, however, we will start on lesson number one. We have just under four hours 'til your required course of sword basics begins, and it's best to get there a bit early."

Ethan nodded and the four lined up, awaiting instruction. Auren was still fidgeting with the top clasp of his jacket, but was paying attention nonetheless.

"First I will have you sit down and cross your legs like this." Edison sat down and folded his legs. He rested his hands on his knees and held his back perfectly straight. "Back straight, Auren. That's great, Stanley," he commended. "Now close your eyes and breathe deeply, in and out everyone." Edison got up and paced back and forth, occasionally making comments to 'relax your arms,' or a reminder to 'keep still.' But soon Auren lost all patience and broke his position, leaning back on his hands.

"Is this *it?* What exactly are we doing?" asked Auren.

"Meditation," replied Edison. "And you gave out rather quickly. It's only been twelve minutes or so."

"My body just isn't built for this," whined Auren.

"Think of it as a personal challenge, Auren — the longer you can hold that position, the stronger you will be to defeat an opponent."

Auren straightened his back and closed his eyes. "I can do that," he murmured.

Several hours passed. Auren was now lying on his back looking at the sky and Ethan had just given up as well. Availia was barely holding on and even Stanley was struggling to sit still.

"That's enough for today. You have forty-five minutes to get to sword basics. It's held in the yard behind the orientation building. After that, another mandatory class taught by me. Stop and get some food beforehand if you wish." He handed the students some coins. "I expect Heinrich will try to wear you out, but save some energy for my class if you can."

"*Heinrich?*" complained Auren.

"Contrary to what you may think, he is a very good teacher — do pay attention."

"Professor … I thought you didn't like Heinrich," challenged Ethan.

"Of course I do," corrected Edison. "But I also despise him — he is my nemesis. I would be lying if I said it didn't please me to infuriate him on occasion. But without him, there would be no challenge to overcome, no adversary to confront — when it comes down to it, what fun would it be without the Heinrichs of the world?"

The four were finishing up meals they had purchased from a cart selling turkey legs. Auren, having finished his long ago, was chewing on some Lippy's brand Lickable Dragon Eggs that he had purchased from the candy store just across the street from MacArthur's hut.

It had been a full day since the news of MacArthur being hauled off to prison. Ethan was wondering if MacArthur was all right, if he would be set free soon and how they would get home. He had difficulty believing he could simply make an appointment with Heinrich. The large-nosed Captain seemed to have quite a dislike for Ethan and anyone he associated with.

"Looks like the class is going to start soon — look, everyone else is wearing armor, well … at least a chestplate," said Auren as he tossed another Lickable Dragon Egg into his mouth. "Here *we* are, wearing jackets that look like pajamas."

"They probly have extra practice armor they'll let us use. Let's just go already," snapped Availia.

Heinrich strode to the front of the group. He wore dark brown leather armor with a black metal chestplate in the center, and a pair of vambraces on his forearms. His hand rested on the hilt of a sharpened practice sword affixed to his belt.

"Today we will get acquainted with the sword," bellowed Heinrich. But he stopped his introductory speech when he spotted Edison's students dressed in their alchemy jackets. "Is this some kind of joke? You dare to show up in my class unprepared? Wearing pajamas nonetheless!"

"*Armor*," mumbled Auren as he tucked the box of Lickable Dragon Eggs into the inside pocket of his jacket.

"Did you say *armor?*" Heinrich drew his sword. Marcus, with a curled lip and a slight grin on his face, pushed his way to the front of the group to watch the display.

"Wait a minute," argued Ethan.

Heinrich stepped a bit to the side and slapped Auren in the chest with the flat side of the blade.

"Ouch!" yelped Auren as he rubbed the spot that the sword had hit.

"Armor indeed. Have a seat over there." Heinrich pointed to a bench several paces away. "Next time, if you don't show up prepared, do *not* bother showing up at all!"

Heinrich went back to the head of the class and disregarded the presence of Edison's four jacket-wearing alchemy students. The instruction went on for two painstaking hours of sword thrusting and defensive maneuvers. Heinrich made all of his students drop their swords and quickly pick them back up to defend themselves. He then paired everyone off and had them repeat everything for the remainder of the class.

"Well, it sure looks more practical than the meditation we've been doing," muttered Auren.

"It sure does," said Availia miserably.

"Hey Availia, I'm really sorry you got involved in all this," said Ethan sincerely. "I didn't mean for you to get caught up in Auren's and my investigation."

"Don't be sorry, Ethan … I'm not," replied Availia. "I know this isn't exactly what I had in mind. I really just wanted to follow my sister's footsteps and make my parents proud. But honestly, if being in the Guard means I have to put up with Heinrich as my instructor, I would rather not. So, let's just focus on getting ourselves in that record department."

"Yeah," agreed Ethan.

"Ngggh ngggh … class is, nggggggggh … over," said Stanley.

The students were dismissed and started gathering at the back of the practice field. Marcus and his group went out of their way to walk past Ethan.

"Did you have fun watching?" asked Marcus smugly.

"Nice pajamas," commented another.

But just then Edison walked by. "Alright then everyone, to the back of the orientation building. Yep, right this way. Marcus, you as well. Ethan, Auren, Availia, and Stanley — what are you waiting for, let's move it," hustled Edison as his class gathered. Meanwhile, Heinrich had another class starting, which meant more swordplay for them to watch. Edison nodded to Heinrich as they taught their classes practically back to back from each other; a slight nod was returned.

"Greetings, students — it's so nice to get everyone gathered outdoors in the fresh air. Everyone have a seat on the ground please, anywhere is fine," said Edison as he motioned with his hand.

"Oh *great*, more meditation," whispered Auren.

"Quiet," shushed Availia.

"This is, primarily, a onetime mandatory course to prepare you for spending time in Tirguard and its surrounding areas. If you look around the class you will notice that most of you are not from Tirguard — some of you are … but most are from Whitehaven. Those of you from Tirguard will also make use of the factual information I will share with you today. I will start by telling you a bit about myself … my name is Professor Edison Rupert. I am by trade a historian of mythology, Mitan culture and philosophy, and the inception of Tirguard."

"A historian?!" whispered Auren in shock. "This just keeps getting better."

"Shhh," snapped both Ethan and Availia.

"In my many years spent in Tirguard I have noticed a very large misconception. It's an easy misconception to make — simply put, that all Mitans are evil hunters of man. There are Mitan who would wish to cause harm to us; but before listening to any rumor and passing judgment, I would recommend experiencing the temperament of the Mitans yourselves."

Marcus sneered at Edison's comments and started whispering to his subordinates. Edison ignored the side conversation and simply continued.

"Now then, let us discuss the typical Mitan, shall we?" continued Edison. "Their bones are more than twice as strong as ours, and can be flexed slightly or made rigid at will. This enables them to jump further, land harder, and exert their bodies more than any human. They are free from defects that could give them or their offspring poor eyesight, deformities, or even baldness," he chuckled. "Some believe this has to do with the mating cycle, which happens every five hundred years. Yes, you heard correct — all Mitan couples have one child per five hundred years — they do not elect out of it. The average Mitan couple will have three children in their lifetime, as they generally live to be two thousand years old. That is an incredibly long time to study history, mathematics, and even the art of combat. Every Mitan should be treated equally as a supreme warrior and a master poet, because they have the time to train for both," he continued. "The Mitans' appearance is very humanoid. The key method for identifying a Mitan is spotting the distinct blue glow around the left eye. Some say these markings glow more profusely in accordance with the future lifespan of the individual, hence, the more brightly the markings glow, the longer the Mitan will live. There are also a few documented cases where the markings were identified as being of a dark purple or almost black glow. We have very limited details on this type of marking. Since the glow makes a Mitan quite visible in the dark — they often wear a mask at night if they wish to avoid detection."

Marcus raised his hand.

"Yes, Marcus?"

"You make them sound superior to us in almost every way. How is a Mitan compared to a Tirguard soldier?"

"That is a fair question. Their dexterity, senses, and reflexes are far superior to any man. So, today … if a Mitan and a human were in a fighting scenario, you could say that one Mitan would be equivalent to five, or possibly more, trained human soldiers."

Marcus was getting annoyed; he leaned over and whispered something to his comrade. They both shook their heads and chuckled.

"You don't believe me?" asked Edison. "Well maybe you'll be the one to change that, Marcus. Now then, I have a small gift for everyone. It's a book with factual information about Losalfar and Tirguard — their history — and other interesting facts. Instead of giving you the book outright, I thought it would be a good time to introduce you to the alchemy vessel. Please everyone draw your attention to the stone basin behind me. If I could just get everyone to form a line, reach into the vessel and pull out your book," said Edison as he motioned the students to stand up. One by one the students reached into the receptacle, paused for a moment, then pulled out a small book. Marcus reached in, snatched his out and walked to the back of the class.

"If you noticed the markings on the side of the basin, we have translated them to mean, 'He who pulls from the vessel is the rightful owner'. As I cleverly placed your names on your book, and meant them to be yours to own, the vessel does the rest."

Auren stepped to the basin and reached in, pulling out a book. He looked into the vessel and checked to ensure Edison was not watching. He then dropped his package of Lippy's Lickable Dragon Eggs into the receptacle. "For later," he whispered to Ethan with a chuckle.

"Hurry along now, Auren, you're holding up the line," snapped Edison.

Ethan stepped to the basin. There was a glowing blue swirl inside, with small specks of light, which looked like stars in the night sky. It appeared to be liquid, but to Ethan's surprise did not feel wet when he placed his hand inside the receptacle. He felt his hand drawn toward an object and clutched his fingers around it. He slowly pulled it from the alchemy vessel. It was not a book.

"A sword!" shouted Auren. "That's wicked!" The sudden shout captured the attention of Heinrich, who was teaching his class just behind Edsion.

"Indeed," murmured Edison as he tilted his head sideways and approached Ethan. The sword was long and thin. It bore a perfect double-edged blade, and yet it was extremely light in weight and felt perfectly balanced. The handle was slightly misshapen in order to accommodate a comfortable two-handed grip.

"I DEMAND TO KNOW THE MEANING OF THIS!" shrilled Heinrich, his face rippling with red and veins protruding from his neck. "Where did you get my sword from, you little…." he growled as he came face to face with Ethan.

"Your *what?* I just grabbed it, I dunno…." stammered Ethan.

Edison interceded. "Easy, Heinrich, the boy pulled the sword from the alchemy vessel. You know the rules."

"You are telling me that this … BOY, pulled *my* sword from the vessel?"

"Yes," replied Edison, now standing between Heinrich and Ethan. "He who pulls from the vessel is the true owner."

"This sword has been handed down from my father, my father's father, and his father before him. Now then," Heinrich reached around Edison, grabbed Ethan's arm and squeezed, "hand it over!"

Edison quickly knocked Heinrich away. The Captain of the Guard looked surprised. He took a step backward as his students gathered around him. Marcus started smiling and pushed his way forward to get a front row seat to the controversy.

"Challenge accepted," announced Heinrich. "Swords only, no alchemy — first to draw blood is victorious."

"Terms?" asked Edison, removing his alchemy jacket and handing it to Ethan.

"For the sword," replied Heinrich as he removed his leather armor and vambraces. "And your terms?"

"Next time you find my students in your class, you teach them as if they were your students, and stop feeling sorry for yourself for not getting them removed from the Electus."

"Agreed," said Heinrich, drawing his practice blade.

"Agreed," said Edison, pushing back Ethan, who was still clutching the mysterious sword.

"What are you doing, sir? You're a retired history teacher!" whispered Ethan.

"Not retired … I was on sabbatical," he smiled.

Heinrich dived forward with his sword leading the assault. Edison quickly drew his sword and blocked the attack. Heinrich advanced, displaying incredible speed. He threw several decoy attacks, twisted his wrist, put all his weight on his front leg and thrust for Edison's sword arm. Edison quickly guided the tip of his blade through his opponent's sword-handle and twisted. Heinrich released his sword and a small drop of blood fell from his finger. Edison held his blade to Heinrich's neck.

"Good match, Heinrich."

"You *cannot* be serious," argued Heinrich.

"The terms are for first blood — one drop should suffice, don't you think?" stated Edison as he lowered his sword and placed it into the sheath. "I believe you have a class with my students tomorrow?"

Heinrich sniveled. "Make sure they show up prepared this time — this is a sword class … not an alchemy class," he snarled as he picked up his sword, sheathed it, and returned to his class.

Ethan's mouth stood agape. "But how did you—"

"Did I mention, while on sabbatical, I joined a retired gentleman's sword-dueling club — works wonders to keep one in shape," winked Edison.

A Predetermined Diversion

"It stands to reason that an assassination attempt on Ethan Wright has just taken place — what would you have me do?!" exclaimed Odin as he slammed his uninjured hand onto the marble table inside the Hall of Kings.

"It's too early, Odin! And sometimes I think you forget your place … remember, you are addressing the King." King Basilius' voice echoed up the tall statue-embossed walls. The short-haired King was in his dressed-down clothes but still bore his father's gold signet ring, with the family crest stamped in the center.

"And sometimes *you* forget, I was placed in charge of Ethan's well-being — I will not stand idly by while an ancient alchemical half-breed werewolf hunts down a mere boy."

"But he's not a mere boy … is he? He is extraordinary," argued the King.

"Extraordinary or not, he has no training! Something about *natural ability* comes to mind," said Odin. He glanced over to Ghislain, who was staring down the King.

"Well, don't look at me! That had nothing to do with the will of Whitehaven. Natural ability was needed to select which brother would go to Tirguard first. That was the will of the Oroborus," exclaimed the King. This comment made Ghislain very uncomfortable. "The Oroborus has a plan for—"

"This conversation is getting out of hand," interrupted Ghislain. "I will not be caught up in any spoken mistakes!"

"The Curse of Silence has ended, Ghislain … which is one of the reasons I called you here."

"Do you know for sure that the entire Curse has ended? I'm not accustomed to speaking of *these things* openly … I know of *those* who died instantly for speaking about *these things!*" yelled Ghislain.

"Perhaps you will find it comforting to know that the Curse ended more than three months ago."

"How do you know that?" asked Ghislain, trying to sound calm but fidgeting with his beard.

"I am the King."

"Yeah … comforting indeed," said Ghislain, leaning back in his chair.

"Ghislain…." sighed the King. "The Curse was never intended to kill any of the families that are exempt, including yours."

"Unless we interfered with the game — with Ethan and the bloody will of the Oroborus! How are we supposed to know what words will or will not interfere? It's best to keep our mouths shut, I'd say. I have a wife and a son! I've seen men die before my very eyes in the pub … they got drunk and started blabbering — you ever seen a man die like that?" asked Ghislain, extremely irritated.

The King looked down at the table and fidgeted with his family ring. Defeated, he looked back up at Ghislain. "One hundred and forty-seven."

"What? One hundred and forty-seven what?" asked Ghislain.

"I have seen, or should I say … I executed … one hundred and forty-seven men. They were convicted of crimes here or in a nearby city … any man that was sentenced to death, once a month, since the day the Wright brothers were born — we would have them recite something that would violate the Curse of Silence … they would simply fall over — dead before they hit the floor." The King looked as if he was guilty of murder. His hands trembled and his face was filled with a look of despair. "The deaths took place every month — until three months ago," added King Basileus. "I was so happy with the man that didn't die after saying the words … I set him free."

Ghislain nodded.

"The day the Oroborus put words in my head … that Curse … was the day I realized there was no other way to know, for sure, that the Curse had ended," said the King quietly.

The room went silent for a moment. Ghislain was satisfied with the explanation and even felt a bit guilty for confronting the King.

Odin interrupted the silence. "The reason we sent Ethan to Tirguard is because the Stonewolf is here. There was no better way to keep him safe."

"And what about *him?*" asked the King.

"Him, who?" challenged Ghislain.

"If you mean Xivon — if he hears that the Curse has ended, he will find a way to reach Ethan, whether it's in Tirguard or here in Whitehaven," argued Odin.

"You have a point, Odin, but I should have been consulted in the matter…." replied the King. "So then … what now?"

"What we need now is a plan," continued Odin. "I was thinking Ghislain and I could train him."

"No — hardly a good idea! I am afraid that is out of the question — no training. Ethan must find his own way; we still must do as the Oroborus willed."

Odin sat silently. He leaned back in his chair and sighed, placing both hands on the table, including the crippled black-veined hand that he normally kept hidden. He looked ready to stand himself up. Ghislain, too, was quite annoyed. Just then one of the tall doors across the hall slowly opened and a well-dressed man walked toward the table. His shiny shoes clicked against the marble floor as he walked, and his overzealous jewelry glistened in the light. It was Tothyll.

"My King," Tothyll bowed. "Ethan Wright is in Tirguard."

"Yes, as I have just been informed. Odin and Ghislain sent him," barked the King. "A bit too early, I may add."

"I just thought you should know, despite the protests of Heinrich, they entered the Electus. Their instructor is a Mr. Rupert…."

This news put a small grin on Odin's face, but the King did not seem amused. "What do you mean, *they* entered the Electus?" asked the King.

"Ethan Wright, Auren Faryndon, Availia Tanbe, and Mr. Stanley … um … — well, they were all selected by Mr. Rupert."

Ghislain was now smirking.

"I am not amused. If he were to join the Guard this early, I wanted him *here*, in *my* Guard! I can keep an eye on him — it's safer," added the King under his breath.

"There's more, my Lord," said Tothyll.

"More?"

"It seems they have found a way to get the alchemy academy re-opened, Your Greatness."

"Did they now?" King Basileus said as he scratched his short dark beard. "Now that is interesting news indeed … although early. Did you say Mr. Rupert as in *Edison* Rupert?"

"Yes, the very same, Sir."

"I was hoping as much — excellent work, Tothyll."

"Wait … you were hoping?" asked Ghislain.

"I made the necessary arrangements long ago, in case Ethan ever went to Tirguard. I placed Edison Rupert on sabbatical in order to have time for tactical training and hand-to-hand combat. He is older, but he knows alchemy like a fish knows water…." The King paused and looked at both Odin and Ghislain intently. "Everything is unfolding as it should — can't be too soon either, otherwise the Oroborus would never have ended the Curse. I mean, doesn't it all make sense now?" The King seemed relieved, as if an incredible weight had been lifted from his shoulders. "Gentlemen, we are lucky to be here at this exact moment. I will watch with an open mind, let events unfold as intended, and watch our chosen saint discover who he is," exalted King Basileus.

"Well said, Excellency," said Tothyll.

"Thanks, Tothyll, now please return to Tirguard and report back any news. Also, let the Castellan know that I will be there in one and thirty to make the announcement about the end of the Curse. I am sure word has reached the city, but an official address is always comforting to the people of Tirguard."

"Yes, my King." Tothyll started to leave, but turned on his heel. "Ah, Sir, one last thing if I may?"

"Yes, what is it?"

"The Castellan had a statue of his father made here, in Whitehaven … and it is ready for display in his hall. With your permission, I would like to take it to him."

"What's the matter, Tothyll, don't they have stone sculptors in the magnificent stone city?" harrassed Ghislain with a chuckle.

"Of course … however, the Castellan's grandfather's statue was made by a sculptor here in Whitehaven. He is quite fond of it, so naturally he wanted this one made by the same man," answered Tothyll with a slight bow.

"Yes, Tothyll, do as you will, I am sure Ghislain is just giving you a hard time. I will see you in one and thirty days," said the King.

Ghislain leaned over and whispered to Odin. "One and thirty?"

"Time difference, Ghislain. Thirty days pass in Tirguard, one passes here," whispered Odin.

Ghislain nodded.

"Yes, my Lord, one and thirty," replied Tothyll. He turned and left, the clicking of his shoes echoing down the great Hall of Kings.

Odin leaned toward the King. "What happened to letting Ethan find his own way?"

The King smiled. "Whatever do you mean?"

"Sending Edison in … re-opening the alchemy academy."

"Just giving him a nudge in the right direction — a … predetermined diversion toward a guided path … if you will." The King smiled and stood up, as did Odin and Ghislain. "It is getting late. I have a room set up for you both; it is best that you stay in case the Stonewolf is still lurking about."

"Not me, Isabel would wring my neck if I stayed out. Besides, if that wolf runs into me, *I'll* bite off more than it can chew," quipped Ghislain. "I will return first thing in the morning."

“I, on the other hand, will stay if it’s no imposition,” accepted Odin. “I’m quite tired, and Wegnel made me promise to take it easy. I even brought his green mystery paste along, just in case.”

“I will have someone show you to your room. We still have much to discuss. I will see both of you tomorrow morning.”

Stanley's Plan

"What do you mean? It's just a handle!" exclaimed Auren, examining Ethan's newly acquired sword.

"No it's not, you daft monkey, it's got two distinct grips on it — you can hold it one- or two-handed," argued Ethan, unsheathing the sword. The morning sun gleamed red on the long, thin, double-edged blade. "It's so light," he added quietly.

"Light indeed," said Edison, walking up to Ethan and taking the sword. He pulled out his spectacles and placed them at the tip of his nose. "I have to say I have always wanted to examine this sword — Heinrich's prize possession, I may add. I'm afraid he's going to be upset for quite a while, Ethan," he added as he handed the blade back. "No dings or anything … it's perfect."

"It doesn't look very sturdy — one tap with a broadsword could break it in half I'd imagine," challenged Auren.

"On the contrary, Auren, I have seen Heinrich use this sword against others and it has never faltered. It's a precise instrument, almost surgical," said Edison as he removed his spectacles and tucked them away. "Ethan, do you have any idea how you pulled Heinrich's sword from the alchemy vessel?"

"No," replied Ethan. "I just reached in and … it was just sorta there in my hand."

Just then, both Availia and Stanley arrived with swords and armor bags.

"Met up with my sister and got my armor, or … her old armor anyhow — should fit. Now we just have to worry about you two," said Availia as she removed the armor from the bag and started trying it on.

"Great, now I'm the only one without a sword," grumbled Auren.

Stanley removed the chestplate from his armor bag and slipped it on. It was black, with blue swirls that shone in the light. There was a silver crest in the center and silver fasteners held the seams together.

"That's right nice! I mean, how did you get it?" exclaimed Auren. "It must've cost a fortune."

"Mmmma, mmaa, my father … mmma, mmma … made," replied Stanley.

"Your father makes armor?" asked Availia.

Stanley nodded and then stared at his shoes.

"Could he make some for us? Or does he have any lying around that we could use, you know, just for Heinrich's class?" asked Ethan.

"Dad's dead," replied Stanley. "Nnngg, nnngggg, sold … nnngg what was … nnngg … left."

Ethan was embarrassed. He put his hand on Stanley's shoulder to comfort his classmate. "I'm sorry, Stanley, I didn't know," replied Ethan. "I mean, I wouldn't have asked, but—"

"It's … okay," replied Stanley.

"Well, let me worry about armor and such for you two," interrupted Edison.

"Sir … where are you going to find armor? We visited every armory in the city," asked Ethan.

"Yeah, everyone's sold out," added Auren.

Edison sat on the ground, seemingly preparing for meditation. "I have until tomorrow, I will come up with something. Besides, I told Heinrich I would have you prepared for class, and prepared you shall be. Now then, you will all meditate for as long as possible. I need to get at least three hours straight today, then we will practice some swordplay."

Ethan sat cross-legged with his alchemy jacket on and fastened the top clasp. Everything went quiet, so quiet he could hear his eyelids when they closed. He saw a flash, and then beams of light. He felt as if he were traveling through the Oroborus.

He opened his eyes. He was standing outside high walls he did not recognize. There was a gate flanked by two trees that reached to the clouds. The walls ran several feet up the massive tree trunks. Ethan was amazed at the intricate design of the wall. The curves and lines fit the tree perfectly, until it was impossible to tell where the tree left off and the wall began. The entire surface was a tapestry of decoration engraved in stone.

As Ethan stared upward, he noticed a platform at the crest of the wall. On top of the platform he saw a figure holding an object. The item was glistening in the light and getting larger and larger. Ethan realized that it was falling directly toward him and he jumped out of the way, hearing a loud crash. Ethan looked back and saw a chestplate, silver in color with a blue crest in the center, lying on the ground. Golden hinges held the seams together and gleamed, even though the armor was resting in the shade of the massive wall.

Ethan regained his composure. As he approached the armor, a second object fell from the wall. It was the figure from the platform. Ethan fell backwards, startled, but sprang back to his feet. The man rose from one knee.

"I am not wearing armor, not today … the only armor I need is precision," said the figure.

A second figure landed on the ground directly in front of Ethan. "But you don't mean to…." he began.

Ethan noticed this man had a strange blue marking on the left side of his face, which was glowing. The first man, who was also adorned with the blue marking, turned and looked past Ethan to address the second. This feature was much brighter and made it difficult for Ethan to concentrate on anything but the bright blue emanation. Ethan now realized this must be a Mitan, not a man.

"If I have to … yes. Enough of us have died, and it's time for difficult decisions to be made. I will carry this burden alone, Hitomi. Do not interfere, regardless the outcome," said the first Mitan.

"But you could lose your light," argued Hitomi.

"Then so be it — there are others…," the first Mitan looked over at Ethan, staring right into his eyes, "…who will someday stand in my place." His eyes were light blue, kind, and very confident. He turned away.

"Loka, wait. All of us stand behind you. We are ready to lose our light," begged Hitomi.

"You are a dear friend, Hitomi, but this is mine to resolve. I will not have anyone else give cause for death today," said Loka with his back turned. He drew his sword and started walking; his pace gradually quickened until he was running. Ethan looked farther ahead and saw an army surrounding them. He thought there must be a thousand Mitan, all with glowing faces. They had been watching the entire time. Ethan suddenly felt dizzy; he lost his balance and fell to one knee. The figures turned to shadows as all light dimmed from Ethan's view.

"Five hours, Ethan! That's fantastic. You see, Auren, just follow Ethan's example," exclaimed Edison. "You're going to be ready in no time!"

"Five hours? But … no, it was only a few minutes," protested Ethan, holding his neck.

"Wow, you were really out of it," said Auren smartly.

"The faces … they were glowing blue. He was going to fight them all by himself," said Ethan quietly. "A thousand of them … while wearing no—"

"Armor," finished Edison.

"Right," answered Ethan, getting to his feet.

"What was his name?" asked Edison. "Was it Loka?"

"Yeah, how did you know?"

"That story is old — very old. What else did you see?"

"His friend tried to talk him out of it. He went to fight them … all of them … all by himself. He said too many had died."

"Indeed, no one knows exactly why he went without armor."

"Loka said precision would be his armor," answered Ethan.

"I love thinking of books while I meditate, although I never heard that version before. Where did you say you read this? They banned those old stories here long ago. I'd be interested in getting a copy if you have one," said Edison eagerly.

"I didn't," replied Ethan.

"I'm sorry, you didn't *what?*"

"Read it … I didn't read it, professor. It was just there. He looked right at me — said that others would stand in his place one day."

Edison's face wrinkled in a display of confusion. He looked as if he were fumbling for his spectacles but did not know why. He found them with his fingers, patted them, and left them in his pocket. "I see," he said as he thought a moment. "Change of plans. There will be plenty of time to practice swordplay in Heinrich's class tomorrow. We will have a test tonight to see how well you have been performing in my class, so prepare for more meditation."

"Oh, man!" complained Auren.

"Go get some rest now, all of you," grumbled Edison.

"Ah, sir?" asked Availia.

"Yes, what is it?"

"I was wondering … well, we were wondering. Other squads are volunteering in different parts of the city. And with you being a historian and all, we thought it fitting that we volunteer for the records department," suggested Availia.

"Yes, that sounds appropriate," answered Edison, still distracted with Ethan's experience.

"Can you let them know to expect us then?"

"Yes, of course," he answered as he started to leave. "I will let them know." Edison walked away still fidgeting with his glasses.

"That was wicked!" exclaimed Auren.

"Yeah, when were you going to tell us about this plan to get us into the records department?" asked Ethan.

"I thought it was best if I kept it from you two. I didn't want to bring it up until Edison was off his guard — didn't want him to get suspicious. You should know this was Stanley's idea."

"Stanley!" congratulated Auren, slapping him on the back. "Great job, you put one over on the ol' professor … and on us!"

"Ethan, are you alright?" asked Availia. "That seemed like quite a deep meditation you had."

"Yeah, I'm fine," he replied softly.

"But wait a minute. So Ethan, you didn't know about this either? Then what was that whole story about the Loka guy for?" inquired Auren.

"I don't know…." answered Ethan.

The First Test

"So all we have to do for this test is meditate … *again?*" asked Ethan, poking his hand through the sleeve of his alchemy jacket.

"Yes, but this is a bit different," answered Edison as he stood over a circular marble basin sunk into the ground.

"Yeah, of course it is. We're sitting on a pile of rocks," complained Auren.

"It's a rock *garden*," argued Availia. "And it's very lovely." Availia had a smile on her face as she looked around at all the small stones that came in many shapes and colors but were roughly the same size. There was a marble walkway leading to, and surrounding, the basin.

"First thing's first!" interrupted Edison loudly. "I want everyone to pick up a stone of their choosing. Select one that best fits you."

"What does that mean?" asked Auren smartly.

"Just pick a stone, Auren. One that fits your personality — something rough around the edges perhaps? Maybe something bold in color. Think about the texture, how it feels when you hold it, how it smells, tastes even…." said Edison as he shifted from one side of the basin to the other.

Auren leaned over and whispered to Ethan. "This is some important rock, eh?"

"Alchemy requires three things to achieve a result," continued Edison. "The first is an element, the second a binding agent, and lastly an alchemist is needed to put them together. Change any of the three, and you will change the expected result — add more and … it gets rather complicated. It is absolutely critical that when selecting a stone, you choose the right one — after today's test, you will carry this stone around with you until you become an alchemist."

The three looked around for their stone while Stanley stood near Edison. Availia selected a small, smooth, round stone. Auren started licking one stone at a time until he found an odd-shaped one that didn't taste as bad as the others. Ethan picked up a perfectly flat, round stone that was dark grey and rather appealing to the eye. He then placed it back in the garden and selected the one next to it. It was also dark grey, smooth, and flat. It would have been round if not for a chunk that was missing from one side. He grasped it in his hand and closed his eyes — he was pleased with his selection and felt he had the right one.

Edison had been paying close attention to Ethan's selection process and observed him discarding the first perfectly round stone.

"Well then, I see you have all selected your stones. Auren, you will go first since it may take you the longest."

"Why would I take the longest? I'm gonna breeze through this test," murmured Auren as he leaned over to Ethan.

"Everyone else can prepare on the balcony over there." Edison pointed to a stairway at the corner of the building. "I will join you shortly."

As the other three students headed toward the stairway, Edison directed Auren to approach the basin. "Okay, Auren, are you ready? Are you prepared to train as an alchemist for reasons of your own choosing?"

Auren looked slightly concerned. "Well…," he thought for a moment, realizing he was doing this to facilitate his stay in Tirguard and help investigate the Stonewolf, "…yeah, I'm ready."

"Good," answered Edison. "Once you sit down in front of this basin, you will place your stone inside it. You will then meditate. Once you have reached a high level of clarity, the basin may reach out to you. If it does, it will fill with water — keep your eyes closed until this happens, or we will be here all night."

"Wait, how will I know if there's water in the basin … you know, if I have to keep my eyes shut?" asked Auren.

"Well that is the question, isn't it? My best guess is, during meditation, you will become one with the basin — you will just know. After the basin fills with water, open your eyes and take the stone," instructed Edison.

"And that's it?" asked Auren.

"That's it."

"And how long will this take?"

"The longest in the history books was just over three days."

"Three days!" exclaimed Auren loudly.

"Just don't peek at the basin and there shouldn't be a problem," replied Edison.

"Yeah, no problem … just have to sit here for a few days, that's all," muttered Auren under his breath. He adjusted his alchemy jacket and looked down at the clasps that remained open. He grasped the stone in his hand, sat in front of the basin, placed the stone inside, and closed his eyes.

Edison joined the group on the stone balcony and discussed the steps necessary to perform the test. They were close enough to see Auren from the balcony, but not close enough to where their voices would carry and disturb his meditation. Several hours passed and the sun started to set. Ethan was lying on the cold floor of the balcony watching for stars. Stanley and Availia were next to him, leaning against the outer wall of the alchemy school. Edison, on the other hand, had been standing the entire time, watching the progress of the meditation.

"How long has he been at it now?" asked Ethan, sitting up.

"About six hours now," answered Edison.

"Do you think he's getting close?" asked Availia.

"It's … rather difficult to tell."

Availia looked over to Stanley. "How long did it take you to pass the test, Stanley?"

"Ngggh, ngghh … dunno, mmmm, mmm … maybe two, nggggh, ngggh … hours," answered Stanley as he shrugged his shoulders.

"It's different for everyone. Over the years, I have come to the conclusion that it's not just the quality of meditation. There are, of course, several known and unknown factors. For example, the type of elements the stone contains, minerals, et cetera. The unknown factors could be many things. Where does the water come from? Do you produce it with your own energy or does it come from the basin itself? Or what about the person, just how ready are they to be an alchemist? These are questions that alchemists of the stone city have asked for years," said Edison.

Ethan got up and stood next to Edison. He leaned over the railing of the balcony to watch Auren, now sitting in the dark.

"Can I ask you, Ethan, why did you pass up the first stone for this one?"

Ethan was a bit surprised by the question. "I dunno. What I mean is … I'm not sure how to describe it, really. The first stone was fine, but the second one was more like me. Almost like … I'm missing something, like this stone is missing part of it. I'm sure it sounds silly, but it felt right when I held it."

"It's not silly at all, Ethan. There are parts to individuals that make them whole, like family perhaps," answered Edison quietly. Ethan nodded.

Just then a brilliant flash of light came from the courtyard, followed by a loud shout of personal victory.

"Yeah!" yelled Auren as he ran through the dark across the courtyard and headed up to the balcony. The three ran down the stairs as Auren was running up. He looked a little stiff from sitting on the marble tile for six hours. "That was intense!" exclaimed Auren.

"What happened? What was it like?" asked Ethan and Availia enthusiastically.

"Well, it was sort of like … I mean … have you ever had a weird dream that was really weird but … you liked it? But it wasn't really like that either — it's hard to explain really," rambled Auren with a huge grin.

"Availia, you are next."

"What, now? It's dark out though," argued Availia.

"Of course it is — but we came here as a group to overcome this challenge. We're not done until we're all successful — no breaks until it's finished. When you have completed the test, you will find us here waiting," said Edison as he motioned her down the stairs.

Availia looked disappointed, as she was already exhausted from waiting for Auren to complete his test. But she quickly took the stone out of her pocket and headed down the marble walkway to the basin. Edison followed Availia down. He lit a small torch near the basin, gave her some instructions, and headed back up to the balcony.

"I don't mind waiting up at all," boasted Auren. "I have loads of energy; I bet I could stay up all night."

Two hours later, the meditation continued. Ethan thought it was fairly obvious that Auren was sleeping, judging by the snoring that was emanating from his mouth. Just then, a flash shot through the sky, accompanied by a quick *BANG*. The noise woke Auren up rather quickly, and he joined the others who were leaning against the balcony watching the event.

"That was pretty quick," said Ethan.

"Yeah, good thing I'm here to stand watch, right?" yawned Auren as he stretched from side to side.

"Yes, Auren, we are indeed lucky," smirked Edison. "Walk with me, Ethan…."

Ethan followed Edison down the stairs, meeting Availia at the bottom. She put her hand on his shoulder and smiled. "I am glad we did this, instead of the Guard," said Availia.

"Let's go, Ethan," said Edison.

Ethan nodded and followed Edison down the dark walkway. The basin was poorly lit, but Ethan could still see wear marks in the marble from previous students that had taken the same test. He pulled the stone from his pocket and clenched it in his hand.

"Remember, Ethan, you need three things to get a reaction. Be one of those things — understand?"

"Yeah, I think so," replied Ethan.

Edison turned and headed back to the balcony while Ethan sat down on the ground. He felt nervous as he reached forward and placed the stone in the basin. He was surprised that it was empty, since Availia had to fill it with water to complete the test. Light flickered on the bottom of the basin, where he could make out the obvious chunk missing from his stone. He took a deep breath, sat upright, and closed his eyes. He felt as if it were the deepest breath he had ever taken in his life. His heart slowed. It was so quiet that he could hear the echoes from his eyelids closing.

Nervousness had subsided. Ethan's mind drifted over past dreams and his family. He could almost touch the future. The stone loomed large as light seeped through the cracks onto the surface of the basin. Droplets of water pushed their way through the bottom of the basin as if it were sweat forming on the skin of a living creature. It filled until the stone was submerged. Ethan felt as if he were watching events unfold in front of him, although his eyes were resting shut. The basin was now entirely full of water.

Ethan leaned forward and reached his hand into the water; it was very cold. He thought of what Edison had told him — he needed to make a reaction. The water grew warmer until it was so hot it should have burned, yet it caused him no pain. Ethan realized it was part of the vision he was having — he focused on controlling it. He concentrated on making the water even hotter, until it started to boil. He leaned forward and touched the stone with the tip of his finger.

Ethan was blinded by light that erupted in a quick burst, and suddenly dimmed. The water in the basin exploded and droplets were flung through the air all around him. They seemed motionless as they slowly drifted past his field of view. It was as if time had stopped to observe this one moment in Ethan's life. He poked several of the droplets with his finger, making them change direction and crash into one another. The basin was now empty except for several water droplets that stuck to the side, and the stone with the crack in it.

As Ethan observed the stone, a small mark carved itself into the shape of a circle. Beams of light emanated from the etching as it was carved, followed by the mark disappearing altogether. Ethan instinctively reached forward and picked up the stone. He opened his eyes.

"Are you alright?" asked Edison in a concerned voice as he leaned over Ethan, now lying on the flat of his back.

"He must've flown twenty feet," whispered Auren to Availia who, along with Stanley, was standing over Ethan.

Everyone looked quite concerned.

Ethan partially sat up. With the stone clutched in his hand he looked up to Edison and smiled. "Never better."

Sword Dueling 101

"And once again, I see some have shown up to my class without the proper gear to participate. But … fortunately for me, this will be the last my time is wasted by Edison Rupert's so-called alchemy squad," sputtered Heinrich. His voice echoed down the Dueling Hall where 'Introductory to Sword Dueling 101' was being held.

The traditional Hall had statues lined up along the walls, all holding up the roof with one hand and stretching a sword to hold up the roof's peak with the other.

"Why don't you two put your armor on? At least you *have* armor to wear; you don't have to get into trouble because of Auren and I," whispered Ethan to Stanley and Availia.

"Yeah," Auren nodded, "Stanley, your armor is wicked! Why don't you use it? No use waiting for us."

"You can't *not* wear armor in a dueling class," argued Ethan.

The veins on Heinrich's forehead pulsated as his face turned several shades of red. Ethan could swear Heinrich had blood vessels popping out from his rather large nose.

"Get out of my class!" shrieked Heinrich. "I have made arrangements to have you banned from Tirguard if you do not complete the standard classes. And you have all failed this class miserably!"

Just then a young man pushed open the giant doors to the Hall, turned around, picked up a large bag and swung it over his shoulder. The girls in the class swooned and blushed as whispers erupted thoughout the Dueling Hall. Even Availia blushed a bit as the long-haired strapping man approached Heinrich. He was strikingly good-looking and was obviously well-regarded, as even the boys in the class were whispering back and forth. The man reminded Ethan of one of the statues lined up along the wall.

"Sorry I'm late," said the man as he placed the giant bag next to Ethan; it clanked as it came to rest on the marble floor.

"And who exactly are you?" asked Ethan.

"I am—" But the man was cut off by Heinrich.

"A distraction to my class — tell me something, Magnus, do you see me parading around the Stadion as you train for your brainless and quite pointless Stadion games?"

"Stadion Champion, yes … *he's* the Stadion Champion, I *knew* I recognized him," whispered one boy. More whispers flooded the vast Hall.

"My deepest apologies, Heinrich, but the city is having its first armor shortage since the Curse of Silence was lifted. I figured if anyone needed—" But once again Magnus was cut off, this time by Auren who was digging in the bag.

"There's armor in here!" said Auren as he pulled a combination leather-and-steel chestplate out of the bag.

"Yes, Auren, a bit bulky I'm afraid, but it should do the trick nicely," answered Magnus with a smile. "On loan, of course," he added.

The girls swooned as Magnus smiled and brushed away the long hair from his face. "You're a fairly strong young man, aren't you, Auren — there was no exaggeration in your father's description."

"You know my *father?*"

"Everyone does. The Mighty Ghislain — only the longest-running Stadion Champion of all time," smiled Magnus as he patted Auren's shoulder.

"The *what?*" Auren yelped in shock.

"Champion of the Stadion … your father — you know. Anyhow, if you find yourself interested in the games, I would be happy to instruct you a bit, just let—"

"That is quite enough, Magnus. Recruit the desperate and insecure on your own time," snapped Heinrich. A snicker came from Marcus Grenwise, pushing his way through the class to get a glimpse of the Stadion Champion.

"Do you mind if I watch for a bit?" asked Magnus politely.

"Oh, why not, this class can't possibly get any worse, can it?" snarled Heinrich as he directed his students' attention to the center of the Hall. "Let us get right to it then. This is a sparring match with an emphasis on defense — everyone who has paid attention or at least *participated* in my previous classes will understand the basics of blocking. Since I have yet to see anything from the famous alchemist foursome, you will go first. I will start with you, Auren, and how about a partner that actually knows what they are doing … volunteers?"

Marcus Grenwise stepped forward. "I'll go," announced Marcus, smirking as he tightened his chestplate and pulled his sword from its sheath. He walked across the marble floor to the center of the ring. The marble outlined a perfect ring and two starting positions, centered underneath the Dueling Hall's peak.

Auren struggled to get the chestplate strapped on properly and was soon assisted by Magnus. "Just keep your guard high and use quick strikes. I hear this Grenwise boy knows the sword quite well, so be on your toes at all times," instructed Magnus.

"Um, I don't have a sword," whispered Auren.

Magnus flicked his two-handed sword from the sheath and caught it by the blade in mid-air. "Use mine," he said, offering the hilt to Auren.

"Whoa, thanks!" exclaimed Auren, grabbing the double-edged blade from Magnus. The sword was quite striking in appearance, which seemed fitting for the Stadion Champion.

Auren stepped to the line. Marcus, who stared at Auren with disgust, backed up to his line and held his sword in ready position.

"Remember, this is sparring only — give and take is key. Ready? Begin." Heinrich lowered his arm and stepped back.

Marcus cocked back his sword and swung with all his might, just missing Auren's middle as Auren flung his midsection backward. Marcus immediately pushed forward and lunged his sword toward Auren's chest. Auren blocked at the last possible second and dashed to the side as another strike came at him. This one aimed wildly at

Auren's unprotected face. He ducked, barely escaping the blow, and leaned forward to shove Marcus back toward the other side of the ring. Marcus lost his cool. He cocked his sword back again and charged. This time Auren was ready and swung back; a soft *ring* came from the swords colliding and several *clank* noises followed shortly thereafter.

"My sword!" yelled Marcus in disgust. "You broke my sword!" Marcus continued to protest as he picked up the other half of his sword from the marble floor. "Do you have any idea how much this cost, you stupid oaf?!"

"I think you paid too much then," retorted Auren as he walked back to hand Magnus the sword.

"That was fantastic, Auren," said Magnus while clapping his hands. The other students in the class followed the Stadion Champion's actions and gave a small applause. This further angered Marcus. He threw the broken sword to the corner of the Dueling Hall where his armor bag rested on the floor.

"That's enough!" shrilled Heinrich in disgust. "Both of you! I said to spar, not take each other's heads off. If you can't control yourself, you will never control a sword. You will both jog laps together until the end of class — fail to do so and you will run laps until the sun sets."

Magnus winked at Auren as he helped remove the chestplate. A scraping sound was heard on the other side of the Hall, where

Marcus slid his armor after his sword. The two reluctantly started jogging together to the end of the Hall and started their laps.

"Ethan, your turn. Since none of you seem to understand the proper etiquette of sparring, you will demonstrate with me." Heinrich's voice echoed through the Hall.

Ethan put the chestplate on as Magnus helped him with the straps. Availia intervened and grabbed Ethan's arm. "No," she whispered furiously. "Heinrich hates you; he only wants to punish you in there. You can't — you simply *can't!*"

"Wait, what are you talking about?" asked Magnus, concerned.

"Well … I sort of pulled his sword from the alchemy vessel, so according to Edison … it now belongs to me," said Ethan as he pulled the sword slightly out of its sheath and slid it back in.

"Oh … that could be a problem, couldn't it," responded Magnus, now with a very concerned look. He turned to the ring where Heinrich was waiting. "Perhaps you would allow me the honor of sparring with you instead?"

"First you interrupt my class and now you want to teach it? Well … no," replied Heinrich bluntly.

Ethan put his arm on Magnus' shoulder. "It's okay … I'll go," he said as he unsheathed the sword and stepped to the line.

Heinrich looked down upon Ethan and glanced at the sword the alchemy student was holding. “Going to use my own sword against me for a sparring match, are you?” snarled Heinrich.

Ethan remained silent.

“Well then, let’s begin,” he added.

Heinrich eased forward and flicked his sword-tip toward Ethan’s chestplate. Ethan pushed his sword forward with both hands to block, but hit nothing. Instead Heinrich pulled back his fake strike, side-stepped, and slapped Ethan’s back with the flat of his blade. Although protected with leather, Ethan felt a sting reverberate through his spine and out his chest.

Heinrich stepped back and waited for Ethan to attack. Ethan regrouped and lunged toward Heinrich’s chestplate. Heinrich made no attempt to move and listlessly slapped Ethan’s advance away with his sword. Ethan was left wide open, but Heinrich did not advance. Ethan swung his blade toward Heinrich’s shoulder, just to have his advance easily deflected again by his opponent. And again, Ethan was wide open long enough that Heinrich could have advanced, but did not. Ethan started low and swung upward, only to have the sword knocked completely from his hand.

“So this is the brother of a coward, is it? You don’t even know how to hold a sword properly — what, do you just spend your time thieving other peoples’ belongings? Have you not paid attention to anything I have taught in previous classes? Pathetic!” hissed Heinrich.

Ethan could hear Marcus snickering as he and Auren jogged past. He was not entirely sure if the sparring match was over, but was so angry he felt the urge to continue.

"My brother is *not* a coward … and *I* am no thief," said Ethan as anger burned in his eyes.

"I am sorry, I don't think I heard you properly … what were you saying?" taunted Heinrich.

"I think that's enough," yelled Magnus, his voice echoing through the great Hall.

The thin double-edged blade lay at Heinrich's feet. He kicked it over to Ethan, who reached down and picked it up. Ethan's anger escalated as he felt blood boiling in his veins. Pulling the dark grey stone from his pocket with his left hand, he held the sword in his right. A blue haze made its way from the tip of the sword down toward the hilt. The blade fogged up, then *clank*! The fog quickly evaporated and the blade started to glow red.

Suddenly, Ethan's scream echoed through the Hall as he recoiled his hand, dropping the sword. He fell to the floor, in excruciating pain, as the skin on his palm blistered and boiled. Smoke came from the marble floor as a charred discoloration made its way around the sword.

"YOU DARE USE ALCHEMY IN MY CLASS?" roared Heinrich. "You're finished here!" he spat.

Lies and Lickable Dragon Eggs

Ethan had been waiting in the infirmary for some time; there were several narrow beds lined up between him and the door. His friends were not allowed inside by order of Heinrich, so he stayed hunkered down in the infirmary bed and waited. The room was quite large and very dark; a small beam of moonlight shone through the window closest to the bed Ethan was lying in. He rolled the cracked stone around in his left hand and tried not to touch anything with his right.

He began to wonder if someone would come in and see him anytime soon, when suddenly he heard voices arguing just outside the door, one of which was Heinrich.

"No! I demand you not only remove him from school, but he be banned from Tirguard altogether!" shrieked Heinrich.

"He is my student, and you can't simply ban him for heating up a sword! It will take time for him to hone his alchemy skills," argued Edison. "Besides, he didn't hurt anyone but himself — and I assure you, that was an accident!"

"He was intentionally attempting to cause injury to me in a sparring match!" spat Heinrich. "It's only a matter of time before he injures another student."

"I was there the entire time. At no point did Ethan attempt injury to you or anyone in the class," came a muffled voice that Ethan assumed was Magnus.

"I am not making any decisions now," said a fourth voice. "And Heinrich, it seems to me that the Captain of the Tirguard armies was in full capacity to defend himself from a twelve-year-old boy, even if he *is* the brother of Isaac Wright. Now then, I will not be bothered with any more of this now. Heinrich, go back to class, and Edison, fetch the nurse. Oh — give the boy back his sword, Heinrich … when it comes to the vessel, you know the rules."

Ethan heard heavy footsteps echo down the hallway, away from the infirmary. He smiled — Heinrich had not gotten his way yet again. The door swung open and in entered a middle-aged woman in a cloak with three metal fasteners clasped at the front. She was carrying the largest cylindrical container of green goop Ethan had ever seen. She sat down in a chair next to Ethan's wounded hand.

"My name is Helga, I will be your nurse," she said as she held out her empty hand. She showed Ethan her palm, and Ethan noticed a strange symbol. "Don't worry, I'm an alchemist. You're in safe hands," she whispered with a smile.

"Is that green stuff from Wegnel … er, MacArthur rather?" asked Ethan.

The woman smiled and rolled up Ethan's sleeve. "No, this is a bit more advanced. I specialize in medical alchemy. Initially we started with MacArthur's recipe, but in this case, we modified it by heating it up."

Ethan looked worried. "Wait, why heat it up?"

"Well, the green paste seems to counteract anything it comes in contact with. If I heat it up beforehand, it will counteract heat — or, in your case, a burn. Like I said, you are in good hands. Let's have you slip your hand in here until it is completely submerged."

Ethan reluctantly slid his hand into the green goop. It felt warm, but instantly provided relief to his hand. Soon it started to tingle.

"There now, is that better?" asked Helga.

"Yeah, it is. Thanks," answered Ethan. "Do you know where my friends are?"

"They were by, but no visitors for right now. You need some rest." Helga slipped a strange lid around Ethan's arm and slid it to the top of the glass cylinder. She snapped it into place and brought Ethan's wrist up to ensure it did not leak. "There now," she added.

"Do you know if my hand will be…?"

"It will be fine, after several days … maybe a week. I will check back on you later and we will take a look. Get some rest now, nurse's orders."

Just then Edison poked his nose in.

"No visitors, Edison," ordered Helga.

"Okay, I just brought Ethan his things so he wouldn't get bored. I'll just set them here. Try and feel better, Ethan," said Edison as he set Ethan's pack down at the side of the bed.

"Edison, is everything okay, I mean…."

"Everything is fine, Ethan, don't worry about a thing," soothed Edison. "Now then, I had better go before the nurse ends up admitting me," he chuckled.

"Do you think Ethan will be alright?" whispered Auren as he unrolled an old scroll. "I mean, did you see the burn marks on the floor?"

"I think he'll be—" answered Availia, but was interrupted.

"*Zut alors!* I said to put the scrolls *away*, Auren, not to read through them!" yelled Madam Kheller as she pulled the glasses from her nose. "Just do as monsieur Stanley does — he is here often and is most helpful." The blonde records woman had been keeping a suspicious eye on them since they walked in. She seemed particularly curious as to why they would volunteer for something as boring as records.

"I think we need to be more discreet," whispered Availia, as she started sorting through the incoming scrolls that were stacked on an inconveniently placed journal desk. She looked down the rows of cubbies that lined the wall all the way up to the ceiling.

"Well, can we hurry up? This place is creepy," complained Auren as he moved some cobwebs from one of the cubbies to put a scroll away. "I mean, this is a nightmare. How are we supposed to find anything about werewolves in this mess?" he asked as he poked at an old statue that was crumbling to dust. As he poked it, half the statue crumbled to form a new pile of dust on an already dusty shelf.

"Wait, Stanley … did Madam Kheller say you help her here often?" asked Availia.

Stanley nodded.

"Then do you know where we can find information on the Stonewolf?"

"Mmmm nnnuugh … no," stuttered Stanley. "Depends — drastically desires dramatic distraction."

"A *distraction?*" asked Availia.

Stanley nodded.

"Auren, go and talk to Madam Kheller for a while — keep her busy!" ordered Availia.

"Why me?" asked Auren. "I don't have anything to talk about. What should I say?"

"You'll think of something, hurry and go before we run out of scrolls to put away."

"Fine then," grumbled Auren, walking to the wooden desk where the beady-eyed woman continued to glare at Availia and Stanley. "Um … hi there," spoke Auren.

"Oui, what is it?"

"Do you have any information on weird creatures lying around somewhere? Like a werewolf … maybe that could have stone skin … or something. Yeah, like a stone-skin werewolf section in here … somewhere," babbled Auren.

The thin-lipped woman stared at Auren with utter boredom. "That isn't the most idiotic thing I have ever heard, so I may be able to assume you are not the biggest idiot I have ever talked to … maybe third … fifth perhaps."

"Are you … being mean?" inquired Auren calmly.

"Oui, I believe I am," challenged Madam Kheller.

"Now's our chance, Stanley," whispered Availia.

Stanley motioned her to the back of the records department. He grabbed Availia's arm and put her in a small wooden chair that looked like a bad replica of the magic chair at Wegnel's, except this one was covered in cobwebs and had a thick layer of dust. Availia immediately tried to stand up only to be pushed back into the seat by Stanley. He put his finger over his lips as if to tell her to stay quiet. He then leaned over and stuck his hand inside the face of an old metal helmet. Availia's chair fell backwards through the wall and dumped her to the other side.

The room was dark; Availia could not see her hand in front of her face. She reached out, felt cobwebs and let out a quick scream. Soon Stanley came through and Availia felt relieved not to be standing alone in the dark.

"Mmmmm, nmmgggu … miracle torch," stuttered Stanley.

"I didn't bring it, it's in my pack," exclaimed Availia as she held onto Stanley's arm.

Stanley walked forward several paces and reached to his left. He picked up a large irregular stone and smashed it against the wall. Sparks shot out and gave him a temporary view of the large room. He evidently saw what he needed to see and walked forward, leaving Availia standing by herself.

"Wait a minute, Stanley!" exclaimed Availia as she stood alone, unable to see a thing.

Availia reached out for Stanley, felt more cobwebs and quickly recoiled. But soon enough the room was illuminated by a torch that had been lit midway accross the room. Confusion washed over Availia as she looked around — Stanley continued lighting torches and it was soon bright enough to see the length of the room. The same cubbies lined the wall, with identical crumbling statues on the shelves and another journal desk positioned in the center of the room. This desk, however, had the stub of a candle sitting on it. Availia could tell it had started out much larger, judging by the wax that had dribbled down the side and onto the surface of the desk. On the journal desk lay a book entitled '*Experimental Alchemy and Derivatives Therein*' that was open to a chapter called '*Prices Paid for Eternal Life*'. Availia realized that Stanley had spent a significant amount of time here. She paged through the book but was interrupted by Stanley handing her a scroll.

"Is this one of the scrolls that Madam Kheller was having us put away?"

Stanley nodded and then walked over to the cubbies that were labeled with the letter '*L*'. He pulled out a scroll and handed it to Availia. She studied both scrolls and looked up at Stanley.

"They are the same," she said, trying to hand them back to Stanley.

"Mmmmm nnngggguuuu … read, nggguuu … again," he stuttered.

"'…realizing my mistake, I was able to free myself from the trap and wound the Mitan soldier. I barely escaped the tyranny of such an evil race of people,'" read Availia aloud. She looked at the second scroll and picked up from the same place. "'*…realizing my mistake, I was able to free myself from the trap with the aid of a Mitan citizen. This isn't at all like what I was told in Tirguard. This Mitan was kind and spoke words of kinship, not tyranny, which allowed me to realize my second mistake.*'"

Availia put both scrolls down on the journal desk and looked up at Stanley. "But, what does this mean? I mean, what is this place, Stanley?"

"Nggguuu, mmmmm … truth telling times to trap troubled … um … mmmm nggguuu … lies," he stammered.

"I don't understand. Do you mean that this room reveals the truth of whatever is placed in the records room?" asked Availia.

"Yes," nodded Stanley, now smiling.

"This could be an extremely helpful room, Stanley, but it doesn't solve our werewolf issue. I wonder how much longer Auren will last with Madam Kheller. Have you seen anything about werewolves in here?"

Stanley shook his head.

"Well, I think we are at a loss for now — we will have to come back later," said Availia, but just as she was about to grab the scroll meant for the records room she noticed a peculiar scrap of parchment sitting on the journal desk. "'Airship is launched by experimental alchemy class,'" she read aloud. "'Red Thomas, head professor of the Tirguard experimental alchemy flight division, accompanied by Stanley VonHaven, designed, built, and piloted Tirguard's very first airship. The airship was considered a success; however, with the eventual closing of the Alchemy Academy, all alchemy items were banned and put into storage, including the airship, which has not been seen since,'" she read.

Availia looked over at Stanley, who seemed to be rather self-conscious about the subject and was avoiding eye contact.

"Stanley VonHaven?" asked Availia.

Stanley nodded.

"So … you built an airship?"

"Nggghhu … yes," he answered.

"That's fantastic, Stanley … I would very much like to see it someday."

Stanley nodded. He then shrugged his shoulders and picked up the scroll that he had just shown to Availia and put it back in the 'L' section. He began putting out the torches.

Availia browsed a bookshelf on her way to the chair, hoping to catch a glimpse of something werewolf-related. She cleared away cobwebs and brushed dust from old books. She noticed an old statue of a man holding a snake in one hand and a sword in the other — a small black band with duel snakes wrapping around had a silver engraving that read '*Mortuus Manus*' and was clasped around the statue's waist. It looked rather odd, so she leaned forward to get a better look when Stanley extinguished the last torch. Startled and now unable to see, she turned and felt her way toward the chair. Stanley reached through the face of the helmet and Availia again fell backward through the wall.

Back in the records department, she could once again hear Auren and Madam Kheller bickering back and forth. Soon after, Stanley fell through the wall. He and Availia scrambled to the small remaining pile of scrolls and placed them in their proper cubbies.

"I have it, mind you, that Lippy's Lickable Dragon Eggs are not *real* dragon eggs, and furthermore, the scrolls here were not, and never *have* been, peeled from the scales of an *actual* dragon!" shouted

Madam Kheller. "Now then, I have been annoyed enough for one evening. Au revoir!"

On the way out Availia looked for the statue of the man holding a snake in one hand and a sword in the other. The remains lay in a crumbled mess on the bookshelf, and the 'Mortuus Manus' band was not to be seen. Availia guessed it had sunk into the dust and crumbles of what was left of the statue. She reached toward the mess but was shoved out by Madam Kheller along with the other two, leaving them with no information regarding the Stonewolf.

Magnificent Stonework

The Whitehaven morning was brisk and Ghislain was irritated by everything around him.

"Your security is annoying, Basileus — bet I could take most of them with one hand tied behind my back," grumbled Ghislain.

"Glad you could join us, Ghislain," sighed King Basileus. "I add extra men to account for the Stonewolf and you still complain about my security? Do you mind if we continue on about the planned protection of our Orobori?"

"Orobori? You'll have to refresh me on your terms, Basileus, we haven't discussed these matters for some time," said Ghislain as he found a chair in the great Hall.

"An Orobori is one chosen by the Oroborus," said King Basileus.

"And…?" prompted Ghislain with a shrug.

"He means Ethan," explained Odin softly.

"Of course he does … why doesn't he just say Ethan then, why does everything have to be so difficult?" murmured Ghislain under his breath.

"Continuing on, then," said the King bluntly. "I have spoken to my advisors and they seem to think the Castellan in Tirguard is well-handed to ensure Ethan's safety. And in further discussion—"

"What about the other three? Auren, Availia, and … Stanley?" asked Odin promptly.

"I didn't ask about them. Although I am positive their safety is implied — but you bring up a good point, considering they are all studying under Edison. I will forward the message immediately," replied the King as he jotted down a message on a piece of parchment. He rolled it up, used wax to seal it, and stamped over top with his ring. An ever-present messenger took the scroll and headed out the door.

"Shouldn't have to worry about Auren, I think he can handle himself — but you know … just to be safe. Probly a good idea," added Ghislain.

The great Hall's door swung open and in walked an old man wearing a purple and black robe. He walked with a cane, slowly making his way to the table. He did not announce himself; rather, he simply sat down.

"Odin and Ghislain, I am not sure if I formerly introduced you to my most trusted advisor," said King Basileus.

"And you still haven't," said Ghislain rudely. "Well, does he have a name then?"

"All of my advisors are named Magnus. This is number seven."

"You can just call me Seven," said the old man. "I have of course heard of you, Ghislain. Your memory is almost as bad as poor old Thomas Wright," chuckled Seven. "The Magnus line has been chosen generation after generation as Castellan to ensure the safety of Tirguard. At age sixty, we step down from Castellan and appoint our eldest son as the new Castellan."

"Then, the retired Castellan returns to Whitehaven to serve as advisor to the King. And because of the time difference, they are about one year apart by the time they get here," added King Basileus.

"As you can imagine, there is great benefit to this arrangement. The King receives a wealth of knowledge, having the complete history of Tirguard at his very fingertips. I am sixty-eight years old, and my son who served as Castellan, Magnus the Eighth, is sixty-seven — his son, my grandson, would have been sixty-six had he not passed away from a weak liver. Out of sixteen total Castellans to carry the Magnus name, thirteen survive and currently serve the King — two have passed, and one looks over Tirguard. And as the King said, all this is possible because of the time difference."

"That is very impressive, Seven," stated Odin. "Tell me, what is advised for the current state of affairs?"

"Well, you cannot advise the path of the Orobori. The only thing you can do is prepare the best chance for success. Although I have great optimism for my line to protect Ethan in Tirguard, ultimately his greatest danger lies in that wretched city. However, since the Curse of Silence has ended, no place is safe for Ethan Wright now, nor will there ever be. Having said that, I think his best chance for success is to become an alchemist."

"I don't think I could have said it any better, Seven," said Odin. "And under Edison Rupert, I have little to fear as long as they stay inside the great stone walls."

"That brings up a good point. I think I will send a trusted advisor to report on the Orobori when he is not with Edison. If he does leave the walls of Tirguard, I want to know about it," stated the King.

"Well, we should be cautious, as this could be seen by the Oroborus as interfering with the natural course of things," replied Seven.

"Of course my advisor wouldn't interact with Ethan — just report back anything of importance. Tothyll is there now, delivering a stone statue of Magnus the Fifteenth — carved by a sculptor here in Whitehaven. I will send word to have him report back on Ethan and give implicit instruction not to interact—"

"Did you say a *Whitehaven* sculptor?" interrupted Seven.

"I am certain I did — we may not be the great stone city, but our sculptors here are—"

"They're dreadful … we need to go to Tirguard immediately! I am afraid your security detail has been compromised," exclaimed Seven.

"What do you mean, Seven?" asked Odin sternly.

Seven was breathing heavily and seemed rather agitated. He leaned forward and slammed his fist on the table. "For generations we have selected the wife of the Castellan from the line of royal sculptors. This line, though unrelated, carries a secret claim to the Castellan position if no son is produced and the Magnus line is broken."

"So out with it then, what is the *point?*" demanded Ghislain.

"By trait they are the royal sculptors, and by law they are to remain in Tirguard to be available to the Magnus line. Their statues are that of legend in the great stone city." Seven paused to catch his breath and continued. "Fifteen had his statue cast by Milt VonHaven … in the VonHaven estate — the statue was completed four months ago … Tirguard time."

"So what did your *trusted advisor* transport that was as large as a Magnus the Fifteenth statue?" asked Odin intently.

The King's eyes widened and his jaw dropped slightly. "The Stonewolf? It can't be," muttered the King in disbelief. He slammed his fist onto the table and rose from his seat. "Organize the entire Royal Guard! We leave for Tirguard immediately!"

A Stone's Throw

Ethan slowly opened his eyes. The room was foggy and dimly lit. He felt like he had just taken a trip through the Oroborus. He was not sure of his surroundings until he felt the jar of green goop on his right hand. Several days had passed since the incident with the sword. He rubbed his eyes with his left hand and refocused. Suddenly, his heart skipped a beat, as three dark figures in black fastened-up jackets were looming over him. Startled, he sat up quickly, attempting to control his panic.

"Sorry we're late," said Availia calmly.

"Yeah, if it weren't for us running into Marcus we would've been here sooner," complained Auren, brushing off the sleeves of his alchemy jacket.

"But if we hadn't run into him, we may not have gotten *this*," added Availia as she held out her palm.

Ethan leaned forward and saw a symbol carved into her skin. It was hard to tell exactly what the symbol was because of the rough, scale-like appearance. He reached out instinctively with his right hand to feel the skin on her palm, only to hear a light clinking noise made by the glass container covering his hand. He reached up with his left hand and felt stone protruding through the skin of her palm.

"That is so weird, does it hurt?"

"No, not at all — just a bit itchy," replied Availia.

"And your jackets," exclaimed Ethan. "They're fastened shut!"

"Yeah, check this out!" bragged Auren as he unfastened the top clasp of his jacket. The rest opened one by one, starting at the top. He pulled his arm out of his sleeve, revealing stone skin that crept half-way up his forearm.

"Marcus got himself a new sword and decided to test it out on Stanley. And … well, Auren jumped in. He and Marcus scuffled, until Marcus took Auren's stone and threw it," said Availia, clenching her teeth.

"And then Availia got angry — it must've activated her alchemy stone, because her hand went all gross and turned to *stone!* So, she used it to break Marcus' brand new sword in half!" hooted Auren as he clapped his hands together. He grimaced in agony as his stone hand slapped into his other hand. He collapsed on the floor as his face turned bright red.

Availia pulled up the sleeve on her jacket to reveal the stone skin ending just past her wrist. "And after we found Auren's stone, his skin changed too — Edison said it's only temporary," she added as she sat down in a chair next to Ethan's bed. "But enough about us, how are you feeling?"

"Good," replied Ethan. "A bit behind you two though. I haven't been able to keep my stone in my hand for very long because I don't have a free hand to pick anything else up," he complained.

"Here," said Availia as she took a glove out of her pocket and slid it onto Ethan's left hand. "Now we just slide the stone inside, and you can still use your fingers."

"Perfect, Availia — thanks," said Ethan gratefully. "So did you learn anything in the records department?"

"Nothing really," replied Availia. "Only that—"

"Only that there is an identical secret room that tells the truth of any document that is placed in records, *and* — the records lady is mean!" spouted Auren.

Availia shot Auren a dirty look and continued. "Stanley was a great help in showing us around, but we didn't find anything on the Stonewolf."

"Well, at least until now you didn't," replied Ethan.

"What do you mean?"

"Your stone skin," continued Ethan. "It's like a temporary version of the Stonewolf's armor. I wonder if that could mean that the Stonewolf was once an alchemist right here in Tirguard."

"A werewolf alchemist?" asked Auren, shaking his head. "That's scary. I wonder if Wegnel knows anything about that."

"Wegnel … er … MacArthur rather — is still in prison. We'll need a bit of luck getting in there to ask him," said Ethan.

"You want to get into the prison?" asked Availia. "How? They don't simply allow visitors, do they?"

"I don't think so — at least not with Heinrich running it. But tomorrow is the Stadion games, and I imagine that most everyone will be there. I think it's our best shot at sneaking in."

A look of immense disgust came over Auren's face. "Wait a minute … I *really* want to go to the games. Do we have to visit Wegnel *then?*"

"Yes!" chorused Ethan, Availia, and Stanley.

That night Ethan was feeling much better. Nurse Helga had said he would be ready to leave the next morning. And with the new glove holding his stone in place, he was ready to examine his map more closely.

When he leaned down to grab the map from his pack, he realized his sword was resting on top. Surprised to see the sword, he stared at the handle and felt as if the sharp burning sensation had momentarily returned. He reached past the handle and dug in the pack, pulling out the map. He quickly glanced at the map, but focused his attention on the material it was made from. He took the corner and stuck it in his mouth. He grasped it with his teeth and tried to tear the corner of the map. It would not tear.

He again reached in his pack, pulling out Wegnel's miracle torch and giving it a tap against the nightstand. A small flame burst out of the top. Attemping to burn the map, he held the flame underneath. It would not catch fire. He gave the torch a tap to turn it off and stuck the end in his armpit. He turned the dial on top of the torch and gave it another tap. Flames shot out, almost a foot high. He held the map in the flames for a few moments. Again, the map appeared to be unaffected. He continued examining the map, subjecting it to any other damage he could think of with no apparent success.

Dim light seeped into the infirmary through the doorway that led to the hall and no light shone through the window. Even after a day of mostly resting, Ethan was getting groggy. With the map still in his hand and Wegnel's miracle torch by his side, his eyes drifted shut and he was soon fast asleep.

Ethan was abruptly awakened by voices coming from the hallway. They got louder, until a shrill scream that carried the very definition of fear filled Ethan's ears. He quickly sat up and peered toward the door.

"Nurse Helga!" yelled Ethan. "Was that you? Is everything okay?" Ethan's voice echoed in the room but went unanswered.

A small rumble could be heard, and like a symphony of thunder from a distant storm, the sound filled Ethan's ears. He checked the window at his bedside to see if a storm was coming, but the night was clear. He heard another rumble, and another. The sound grew louder and Ethan realized that giant footsteps were approaching the infirmary. The booming echo came closer and closer until it suddenly stopped right outside the door.

Ethan fumbled for his map, grabbed his miracle torch and jumped out of bed. He tried to remove his injured hand from the jar of green goop, but the jar was stuck at his wrist.

Suddenly, the door flew open and crashed into the wall. The top hinge ripped off completely, leaving the door hanging crooked against the wall. The light from the hallway blinded Ethan for a moment. He realized that he was now staring at the shadowy figure of the giant Stonewolf, just a stone's throw away.

The beast's chest heaved in and out as drool flung out from every exhaled breath. The Stonewolf stepped into the infirmary, ducking its enormous head under the doorway as it entered. It appeared to be wearing a new pinch-shackle — this time attached to the creature's neck. It looked directly at Ethan with its one giant yellow eye. The other, still injured from Loki's attack, was swollen shut and looked agonizing. It clenched its jaw, grinding its teeth from side to side as if preparing to feast.

Ethan froze for only a moment. The wolf charged through the infirmary, shoving empty beds from its path. Ethan quickly slammed his miracle torch against the nightstand, igniting a colossal flame. The Stonewolf was surprised and halted momentarily. Ethan smashed the jar of green goop against the nightstand, flinging glass and jelly-like paste everywhere. Fending off the Stonewolf with the miracle torch, he leaned toward his pack. With his jelly-covered hand, he wrapped the map around the handle of his sword and pulled it from its scabbard.

"STAY BACK!" yelled Ethan, swinging the torch at the creature.

The wolf snapped and growled as it tried to find a way around the flame coming from the torch. The sword made a *CRACK*, and streaks of blue glided down the blade. Heat was radiating through the creases of the map. Ethan swung the sword tip toward the wolf, holding it as far away from his body as he could. More heat poured from the handle, becoming almost unbearable on Ethan's eyes and face. The wolf sensed this heat as well and backed up several steps.

Ethan had to act now, or risk dropping the sword altogether. He quickly swung the sword over his head and with all his might, lashed it toward the Stonewolf. A thin line of molten fire extended from the blade like a whip, hitting the beast across the face. It recoiled; quickly covering the resulting wound, the beast howled and bolted out of the infirmary on all fours.

Ethan gave a sigh of relief, and the sword gradually began to cool. His jagged breathing started to slow. He released his grasp on the sword and it clanked against the stone floor of the infirmary. He shoved the map in his pocket as the goop on his hand gave off whirls of smoke, smoldering from the heat of the sword. Slowly dripping from his fingertips, the green paste cooled instantly as it made contact with the stone floor. Still in shock, Ethan refused to release his gaze from the spot where the Stonewolf had stood. Hearing a hiss, he realized the flame was still shooting out of his miracle torch. Without breaking eye contact with the doorway, he leaned over to the nightstand and gave it a small tap, extinguishing the flame.

Just then Heinrich rushed through the doorway. Seeing the door hanging from its hinges; a thin line of molten fire smoldering on the floor, wall, and one of the infirmary beds; glass smashed all over the floor; and green goop everywhere, Heinrich exploded.

"WHAT THE HEL? I don't even know where to begin! You destroyed yet another floor? I will have you for this, boy!" he roared.

Just then the bed that had been smoldering collapsed in two. Heinrich charged forward, grabbing Ethan's arm. "You're coming with me."

Ethan was pulled down the hallway and shoved into a room on the left, where several people were gathering. Heinrich quickly attempted to make his presence known.

"General Lodbrok!" yelled Heinrich through the havoc. "General Vacheal Lodbrok! I seem to have found the source of all the commotion. It seems that Mr. Wright took it upon himself to destroy yet *another* piece of historically significant property," announced Heinrich. His voice was barely louder than the bickering of Nurse Helga, the rambling of Edison Rupert, and Madam Kheller who was babbling frantically to the General.

"I'm sorry, what's this?" asked the silver-bearded General, motioning with his hands for everyone to be silent.

"I discovered that Ethan Wright has destroyed half the infirmary! It appears his alchemy training has gone awry. As I protested earlier, the boy should be banned from Tirguard."

General Lodbrok looked over at Ethan.

"Explain yourself," commanded the General.

"Ethan didn't cause this!" interrupted Nurse Helga. "A horrible-looking wolf came down the corridor when I was doing my rounds. I locked myself in this office — barely able to escape the creature," sobbed Helga. "It was headed toward … the infirmary … toward Ethan!"

"And what did you see, Ethan?" asked Edison calmly.

"Um, I was resting and I heard a commotion. Then, the Stonewolf came into the infirmary. I used the sword to try and scare it off. I ended up hitting it in its—"

"Face?" pressed Edison anxiously.

Ethan looked surprised. Heinrich looked even more surprised.

"Don't worry, Heinrich, the City Watch has been notified. And it was reported back that the Stonewolf has managed to scale the city walls and escape. It appeared to be injured across the face — thanks to Ethan … and thanks to alchemy, the beast fled," added Edison sternly.

This was the first time Ethan had ever seen Heinrich look embarrassed.

"That school is an abomination to the name *alchemy!* It was closed for good reason, and should remain closed," snarled Heinrich, but his protest went unregarded.

"You are one of my most trusted men, Heinrich, but I take orders from only two people — King and Castellan. I give orders to all else ruled in Tirguard. There is nothing you can do about the alchemy school reopening — it's here to stay by order of the King, so come to terms with it. If you wish a student under the school of alchemy to be punished, Edison is Captain — talk to him … not me," stated General Lodbrok.

"Captain?" argued Heinrich, stomping his foot.

"Of course," said the General. "You're Captain of the Guard, and Edison is Captain of any student of alchemy in Tirguard — which makes you equally ranked. So if you could discuss your quarrels with him instead of me … that would be appreciated."

"He has four students under him — that hardly makes him a Captain!" exclaimed Heinrich.

"Do you desire him to be Captain of all students, Guard included?"

Heinrich appeared to choke on his own spit momentarily. He snorted and huffed. "No, General, that will not be necessary," surrendered Heinrich reluctantly.

The Stadion Distraction

The crowd *booed* as a spear stuck into the ground just shy of its mark. But as Magnus entered the arena, the crowd in the great Stadion cheered so loud that Ethan thought the giant stone walls would shake apart.

Ethan and Auren made their way up the stone staircase just inside the Stadion walls — they looked around for where Stanley and Availia might be sitting. Not finding their classmates, they followed another set of stairs that went halfway to the top of the wall, ending at a small doorway. A short, red-bearded fat man standing by the doorway noticed the boys and ran down the stairs to approach them.

"Aye, you there!" He was vertically regressed due to age, wearing a silly hat and small, stylish spectacles.

"Us?" asked Auren.

"Yeah, you, I need a really big favor from you — can you follow me up here, please?"

Ethan looked at Auren; the man did not seem threatening at all. He looked, in fact, sort of silly.

"Please, I'm kind of in a jam here, I just need you for … seventeen seconds … please?" pleaded the man again. He seemed very desperate, so the boys gave in and followed him up the stairs and through the door. They realized they had walked into an announcer's booth.

"What is *this?*" asked Ethan, but was barely heard for the roaring of the crowd.

The fat man leaned into an elaborate mouthpiece that led to an enormous funnel. In a very deep, loud voice he bellowed out to the masses, "Ladies and gentlemen!" The rumble of the crowd grew much louder. The portly man paused to let them cheer for a while.

"Ladies and gentlemen, do I have a treat for you on this most glorious day. I don't want to be without a proper introduction so let me say, I had an epiphany — a grand idea that tops *all* grand ideas. To introduce the first event, better late than never, I have none other than the grand marquis of wisdom, the warrior for those who find themselves shrouded in peril — the very brother of Isaac the Virtuous. Show your love today for none other than … *Ethan Wriiiiight!*" The announcer looked over to Ethan with a grin and motioned for him to come to the funnel device. Ethan did not want to go at all, but with a shove and a grin from Auren, he stepped up to the fat man.

"A favor, huh?" Ethan whispered to the man. "What do I say?"

But the red-bearded announcer ignored him and stood back. Admiring the adulation from the crowd, he took a bow.

Ethan crept forward, stuck his face near the device and mumbled, "Uh, let the event begin." The first part squeaked out, but the audience did not seem to care; they roared with anticipation and Ethan took a few steps back.

As the plump man was clapping he said from the side of his mouth, "Brilliant, kid, they love you."

"What was that about?" asked Ethan.

Auren leaned into Ethan. "So much for keeping to ourselves," he laughed.

The announcer ignored them and the first event got underway. Ethan and Auren watched intently as armored men took turns throwing spears. Ethan noticed that Auren's eyes were riveted on the action below.

"Makes the youth sword competition look pretty small, huh?" asked Auren.

"Yeah, this place is huge!" exclaimed Ethan.

The bespectacled announcer glanced at Auren. "Hey, you look familiar too, do I know you?"

"I don't know," replied Auren, not breaking his concentration.

"Well what is your name, lad?"

"Auren … Faryndon," replied Auren.

The fat man's eyes grew in size. "In many many years, I never would have thought…."

The event came to an end and the man rushed to the speaking device.

"Now that was fantastic!" The Stadion resounded with the cheering of the crowd. "Give some applause to our exhibition champion from our own Tirguard, Tranhom Welton!" The crowd grew even louder and he paused for them to finish. "Now then, you did not expect to come here today and see Ethan Wright, but Ethan you saw, and he amazed you with his ground-rattling announcement; but what would you folks do if I could warm your hearts?" He paused and the crowd thundered. "What would you do if I could rattle your bones?" He paused again, and again the crowd cheered. "And what would you do if I told you that here today, in this very

Stadion, we have the son of the mightiest Stadion Champion in existence? Pound your hands for Auren Faryndon, son of *GHIIIIISLAAIIIIIN!*"

Ethan had never heard anything this loud before. The audience was pounding on the wooden rails and stomping their feet, all the while shouting at the very top of their lungs.

Auren had jumped upright and seemed to be in mortal shock. He stood there looking at the crowd with a blank expression.

The red-bearded man leaned over to him. "You got anything to say, boy?" Auren stood there motionless with his jaw hanging open. The tubby man waited for a reply but none came. "Well, just wave then," he added kindly. Auren lifted a hand and waved to the crowd. The cheers and applause came quickly, followed by chants for Auren and Ghislain. The noise was so loud that Auren could not hear Ethan, who was standing right next to him.

When the crowd finally settled down Ethan leaned in to talk to the fat man. "Who *are* you, anyway?" he asked.

"Oh my, I do apologize, boys. I am Red, the announcer for the great Stadion."

"How do you know my brother?"

"Firstly, kid, who *doesn't* know him? And secondly, you look just like him … I mean, it's uncanny."

"Actually," started Auren in his smarty-pants voice, "he looks *exactly* like him."

Ethan waited for a moment, expecting to get a better answer from Red, but soon realized that none was coming.

"It's just that, well, I'm looking for him. We were hoping you could tell us something … maybe where to find him?" ventured Ethan.

"Well, I haven't seen him around here in ages, but I know where you could start — Losalfar."

"Can you tell us how to get to … Losalfar?"

"Sure, just go out the North Gate, down the path, through the woods, head north and try to avoid certain death. It's about two days' hike — can't miss it."

"Wait, did you say certain death?" asked Auren.

"Yep, pretty sure I did."

"Is there any way to get there without the *dying* part?" asked Ethan.

"Yeah, I'm kinda interested in skipping that as well," smirked Auren.

"I'm sure there is, lads — but most here in Tirguard try their best to stay inside the walls. You should do the same. Now then, thanks for helpin' me out with the announcement today — and hey, stick around and I'll have you meet some of our *mighty warriors*," added Red in his deep announcer's voice.

Not a moment had passed, when one of the Stadion Champions came up the stairs behind them.

"Greetings, glad you could make it," said a familiar voice.

"This is Magnus the Grand, for he has been our defending Stadion Champion for many years now," announced Red as if he were addressing the audience.

"Yeah, we already sorta met," answered Ethan. "Thanks for bringing us armor. You saved our skins from Heinrich."

"I'm glad I could help. How's the hand?"

Ethan held his hand out and flipped it to show Magnus both sides. "It's good," he answered.

"I'm glad you're feeling better. When I heard the announcement that you were here, I wanted to make a proper introduction. Auren, I hold the very highest respect for your father; he has set records that *to this day* have not been broken. I could only hope to be half the champion he was," said Magnus humbly.

"Oh…," replied Auren. "Well … that's my old man…." Auren was relishing the fact that he was getting much of the attention, instead of Ethan.

"I was wondering … would you care to come down and give the spear a hurl? It would do me great honor to have the son of Ghislain out to—"

No sooner did the words leave his lips when he was interrupted by Auren. "*Would I?* Of *course* I will!" he exclaimed, with an excitement that Ethan had never witnessed in his friend.

Magnus led Auren down the steps and they entered the floor of the grand Stadion. It was not long until Auren heard the bellowing of Red, yelling to the crowd what was about to take place. Hearing the announcement, Auren began to get rather nervous.

"Ah, Magnus, I haven't … exactly thrown a spear before," confessed Auren, embarrassed.

"No problem, Auren, this is only an exhibition, so no pressure," said Magnus as they approached a weapons rack. He took one of the polished metal spears and handed it to Auren. "It's easy," he added.

"Light," said Auren in a surprised voice.

The spear was very long and felt awkwardly balanced. Magnus, too, had taken a spear and Auren saw that he was holding it by what appeared to be a notched-in handle. Auren shifted his grip to mimic Magnus, and suddenly felt the balance right itself.

"Yes … light in weight, but very effective," said Magnus, who now had Auren's attention. The Stadion Champion began to give him a rundown of all the rules.

"Now then, the circle we are standing in is called the starting ring; you may not leave the starting ring until you have released the spear or you will throw dead, which means you forfeit your turn. There is a wood-framed rectangular target on that side of the field," Magnus pointed to the other end, which seemed an impossible distance away.

"That box is called the Pyxidis, and the key is — well, the key is to hit the Pyxidis if you can. If you do hit it, you get five points. Now then, around the Pyxidis is a wood-framed square. This is called the Archa. Hit inside the Archa and you get three points. And around the Archa is a large circle, which is called the Rail. You don't get any points for getting inside the Rail, but you earn one and only one extra throw. Do you follow so far?"

Auren was a bit overwhelmed, and confident that he would be unable to reach any of the boxes or circles Magnus had pointed to, so he just nodded.

"Great, you get three tries. I find it works best if you take a few steps and lunge it as hard as you can. Keep in mind this contest is as much about accuracy as it is about strength. Are you ready to give it a try?"

Auren nodded again and Magnus took a few steps backward to give him some room. Red, of course, took this chance to announce 'Auren, son of Ghislain's' first attempt. This made Auren's stomach tie into knots, but the cheering of the crowd reassured him. He took three giant steps, leaned forward, and plunged the spear straight into the ground about ten paces away. The crowd was unrelenting; half were laughing and the other half hooted and booed.

Magnus approached with another spear. "Don't worry about Red and the crowd, I can see you are very strong so just aim a bit higher — your form wasn't too bad."

Magnus backed up again, giving Auren space to throw. Red bellowed out that Auren was going to attempt a second try. Auren thought to himself that this was very difficult to ignore, for the chunky man had an extremely deep and loud voice. He gripped the spear tightly on the notched handle, took his three steps, leaned forward and hurled the spear. This time, even to his own surprise, he let out a loud *grunt* while releasing the spear. This seemed to help, for it went much higher. But a few seconds later, the crowd grew quiet. The spear sailed right over the Pyxidis and was heading for the stands. A small crowd of people dispersed and the spear impaled a wooden bench, wobbling a bit as it stuck.

Ethan, who was still watching from above, looked over to Red who was strangely silent. "Ah, Red … is that supposed to happen?" he asked.

"I … don't know," answered Red in an abnormally quiet voice. "Never seen that one before."

"Have you ever seen such strength!" bellowed Red to the crowd.

A few moments passed as the spear swayed back and forth and then the crowd erupted into cheers. Auren was not sure what the cheers were for; it seemed obvious to him that he could have impaled one of the spectators. He assumed he would be done at this point, but Magnus approached with a third spear.

"Are you sure…?" but Auren was interrupted by Magnus.

"We're lucky this isn't a distance competition. You may want to concentrate on accuracy and not so much strength. Give it a bit more arch this time."

Again, Auren nodded. Red was announcing the third and final throw. This time Auren could see some of the spectators moving from the path of another possible spear landing in the stands.

Auren made his approach and released the spear. Again he grunted, but this time he aimed much higher and the spear sailed far above the Stadion. Magnus walked over to Auren while trying to keep an eye on the spear.

"Not sure about that one — did it get away from you?"

Just then the spear drove itself deep into the very edge of the center box, sending a small cloud of splinters in every direction.

"Oh, you hit the Pyxidis, that's five points!" exclaimed Magnus as he patted Auren on the shoulder. "Not too bad for your first time out."

The crowd was in an uproar as they cheered out Auren's name. Red was saying something, but even his loud bellows could not overpower the cheers of the crowd. Auren gave a wave and made his way off the field alongside Magnus.

Ethan looked back over to Red, who was now sitting down and wiping sweat off his forehead. "You just can't get much better than that, my boy," said Red, sounding exhausted.

Soon Magnus and Auren returned to the announcer's room where Ethan and the tubby man were waiting.

"Thanks again, Magnus, that was *incredible*," said Auren with a huge smile on his face.

"The pleasure was all mine," said Magnus as he shook hands with both the boys. "If you boys need anything, please let me know. But now I have to get back before the next event."

"So much for keeping a low profile," said Availia as she came up the stairs, with Stanley just behind her.

"Well, if everyone thinks we're here … we should have an easy time sneaking down to the prison," plotted Ethan.

The four snuck out of the grand Stadion unnoticed and headed toward the spire, home to the one man Ethan wished to avoid that night.

"I don't see any light coming from the window," whispered

Auren.

"Maybe Heinrich isn't around," replied Availia softly.

"Well, hopefully he isn't at the prison then. Stanley, are you sure the prison is just below the spire?" asked Ethan, now worried that his plan was in possible jeopardy.

Stanley nodded intently.

"Well, let's go then," Ethan motioned.

They followed Stanley to a building across the street from the spire and stood behind him as he peeked around the corner. As Ethan looked around the corner, Stanley pointed to a ramp that led down to a small wooden door that was the prison entrance. There were chairs on either side of the door, with guards sitting on each chair.

"Guards? Terrific … Stanley, you didn't say anything about guards — we'll never get in there now," grumbled Auren.

"No, wait!" said Availia, peeking around the corner. "There's something wrong with them," she added as she stood up and walked toward the entrance.

"Availia, wait!" exclaimed Ethan.

The three boys shrugged their shoulders and reluctantly followed Availia to the prison door. Both guards were unconscious and positioned in their seats so as not to fall over.

"Not sure if we should be here, it would look bad if we got caught," said Auren. "We could always go back to the Stadion and finish watching the events."

Auren's protests went unnoticed.

Ethan marched forward and pushed the wooden door open. The others followed him as he walked down the torchlit hallway. It smelled like sewage and mold. They passed several empty cells before they reached the end of the hall and turned the corner. The iron doors were just large enough to stuff a person through, but the prison walls, like the rest of Tirgard, were thick stone. Ethan stuck his nose between the bars of several cells, until he found a cell with MacArthur huddling in the corner.

"I would surmise that Heinrich didn't just let you in here to visit," groaned MacArthur. He pushed himself up off the floor and limped to the iron door. He looked scruffier than usual, reminding Ethan of what Wegnel looked like in his normal state.

"No, we snuck in," answered Ethan. "How are you?"

"Not good, my boy. Being so far away from the Oroborus, I am already starting to merge with my counterpart. I feel as if I am going to lose it…." MacArthur sniffed, then regained his composure and continued. "Wegnel is most likely going mad at this point, I can start to feel his thoughts — he's scared. I don't have much time," exclaimed MacArthur desperately. He reached his hands through the bars and pulled Ethan close. "When I was first bound to the creature

… Dimon, he said I could ask him a question — any question."

"What did you ask him?"

"I asked him why we are here… why do we *exist?* He said, 'that's easy — because the conditions were right.'"

Ethan tried to back away but was pulled in closer.

"Ethan, you must listen to me very carefully," whispered McArthur frantically. He seemed urgent as he tried to catch his breath. "There is a natural progression to life — seven worlds — each a progression from one life to the next — humans, Mitans, Airmoor … it's all the same — one big Game, Ethan … played … one Oroborus versus another — a grand game of chess. You are important, Ethan … you mustn't let Xivon know you're here. He's the most dangerous Mitan in this world and is bent on seeking you out. And once again, the conditions are right — you can win this Game!"

"I don't know what you're saying, MacArthur. I need to find my brother!"

Suddenly a voice echoed out directly behind them. "What are you doing here?!" yelled Edison, carrying something that looked like one of Wegnel's miracle torches.

"We need to find out about the Stonewolf," answered Availia quickly. "We came to find out why it has stone skin."

"It has stone skin because it was an alchemist from Tirguard. Being a historian, I could have told you that without you breaking into a prison. Do you realize how much trouble you could be in? I can't hardly explain this one away, now can I?"

"What about the guards out front, can you explain that?" challenged Ethan rashly.

"They'll be fine. Just some Lippy's Concentrated Sleep Sauce in the guards' tea — they'll be over it by morning."

Edison pushed past Ethan and peered in the cell. "You don't look so good, my friend."

"I've been better," replied MacArthur. "Wegnel, I fear, is in far worse condition."

"Will you merge soon?" asked Edison.

"I still have some time, Edison — more importantly, I overheard Heinrich earlier. They are going to start a war … tonight."

A look of worry came over Edison. Sweat rolled down his forehead and his face went pale. He refocused on MacArthur.

"I had a suspicion this would happen after the Curse of Silence ended … what do we do?" asked Edison.

"Heinrich talked the Castellan into sending an army to Losalfar. And in an attempt to avoid panic throughout the city, they are using the Stadion event as a distraction to send the army out as we speak."

“Is Heinrich with them?” whispered Edison.

“Yes, he and General Lodbrok are leading the attack.”

Edison backed away from the bars. “I’m going to Losalfar tonight — you will all have to work on getting MacArthur free from prison and back to the Oroborus.”

“We’re going with you,” announced Ethan.

“You most certainly will not,” snapped Edison, who was in no mood for arguing.

Ethan stepped forward and looked Edison in the eyes. “There is a chance I can find my brother in Losalfar — there is nothing you can do that will change my mind from going.”

Auren stepped forward. “Me too,” he stated.

Availia and Stanley stepped forward as well; she glanced at Stanley and back to Edison. “Us too.”

Edison stumbled over his words and gasped in trying to find a protest, but none came. “Fine then!” he exclaimed. “You will just go … and simply stop a war from taking place, while I work on freeing MacArthur. But I’m not allowing you to travel there alone. If we do this, it will be done my way!”

A Familiar Face

"How do you know the torches will be lit? I can't fly this bloody thing in the dark," exclaimed Red as he unstrapped the airship.

"They will — Mitans are meticulous about these things," reassured Edison as he started removing ballast from the front deck.

"What?" exclaimed Auren. "You want us to get in an airship?"

"You'll be fine," answered Edison. "That is, if this still works … and I am sure it will work as expected, most likely," he added under his breath.

"With him?" protested Ethan, now pointing to Red. "The Stadion announcer — as the pilot?"

"Well in my defense, I wasn't always a Stadion announcer," retorted Red as he removed additional ballast from the rear deck.

"We don't have time to argue," grumbled Edison. "Stick to the plan and you'll have the best chance for success."

"Red, you and Stanley built this airship, didn't you?" asked Availia.

"We sure did, one of the best things I've ever done and not allowed to talk about," said Red as he threw one of several levers located in the center of the ship. A *whoosh* was followed by fire that could be seen shooting through a chamber and up into the balloon; a few seconds later the airship started to lift off the platform.

Edison smiled at Availia. "It works!"

"Everybody on," ordered Red as he unlatched a small staircase which swung down to the platform. "I want to get off the ground before anyone notices."

Ethan, Auren, Availia and Stanley boarded the airship. Edison stayed behind and started untethering it from the platform.

As the airship started to rise, Red leaned over the edge where Edison was standing. "If I get *murdered*, I will haunt you for eternity."

"You already do, Red," quipped Edison as he waved them off.

The airship rose quickly over the city. Stanley and Availia walked to the back deck to look around. Red was adjusting knobs and levers in the middle of the ship while Auren and Ethan leaned over the rail to watch the ground get farther away.

"Tirguard is amazing," said Ethan.

The walls of the great city could be seen by the torches lining the stonework. Ethan could see that the walls spanned around the great spire that housed Heinrich and stood atop the prison. A second, smaller, wall stretched around the market district, containing the hut which was home to MacArthur and the Oroborus.

The great stone city got smaller as the airship rose into the night sky. The air started to get chilly the higher they flew. Ethan's hands started to get cold, so he stuffed them into the pockets of his alchemy jacket. He had never seen an airship before, let alone flown in one. So when the balloon that was lifting the ship shuddered and they suddenly dropped several feet, a panic ensued.

"WHAT WAS THAT?" screamed Auren, who was turning pale.

"Just turbulence — all is fine … probly best to have a seat for a while!" yelled Red over the noise of the wind as he continued to pull on levers and adjust knobs.

"WHAT?" yelled Auren as his ears began to pop. He stuck his finger in his ear and wriggled it back and forth to clear the pressure.

Ethan took a seat next to Auren. "Pretty amazing, huh?"

"I think I'm scared, Ethan," admitted Auren quietly.

"Me too," replied Ethan. "I wonder what they'll be like … the Mitans, that is."

Auren's face was even more pale than before. "I didn't even think of that. Just trying to get past the 'sailing through the air' part of this trip, or as Red calls it … *certain death.*"

"I don't think he'd be with us if it was 'certain death.' I'm pretty sure he meant if we walked to Tirguard — I think you just need a distraction."

Ethan reached into his pack and grabbed the map. "Here," he said as he shoved it into Auren's hands.

Auren tried to examine the map, but it was difficult to see in the dark. Ethan lit his miracle torch and held it in front of the map for Auren to study.

"It looks like Tirguard," exclaimed Auren.

"I know," said Ethan. "My father left it for Isaac … I think it may help me find them."

"You should show this to Professor Rupert, he probly would know—"

"No," interrupted Ethan. "I can't show it to anyone just yet. There's something strange about this map I need to figure out first. Watch."

Ethan held the torch under a corner of the map. Auren instinctively recoiled, but Ethan grabbed Auren's arm to hold the map steady as he demonstrated that it would not catch fire.

"WHAT?" exclaimed Auren with a look of utter disbelief. "That's impossible!"

"What are we talking about, boys?" said Red as he came around the corner.

Ethan quickly released Auren's arm, and Auren responded by stuffing the map in his inner pocket.

"Nothing," said Ethan and Auren in unison.

"Good. Can you put that torch away then? I don't want anyone to spot us up here. I think we are high enough now — time for our little airship to run silent," he said as he pulled another lever. The fire in the chamber suddenly dimmed and the whooshing sound decreased. He then pulled a large black curtain down the length of the ship.

Ethan quickly put out the torch and put it back in his pack. He supposed the curtain would make them more difficult to see from the ground and hide them in case they passed over the Tirguard army. But more importantly, the curtain also kept the wind off them.

"It's beautiful up here, isn't it?" said Availia, making her way to the front of the ship.

Ethan had been so distracted by the sight of Tirguard that he had forgotten to take a good look around. He looked up at the stars and across the horizon. It was indeed a beautiful sight. He felt comfortable on the airship, like he belonged in the sky, like he was meant to be there. As he looked around he noticed Red smiling at him; Ethan smiled back. Soon Stanley joined them at the front of the ship, and the five of them sailed through the air together — they had the sky all to themselves.

Several hours had flown by. Auren was now sleeping on the deck of the ship. Availia and Stanley were still enjoying the view, but starting to tire.

"So how does the ship work?" asked Ethan.

"Well, you're an alchemy student, aren't you? What three things are needed to make a reaction take place?" challenged Red.

"Um, well … the first thing is an element of some kind … the second, a binding agent, and the third thing is…." Ethan tried to think, but could not remember the third thing.

"An alchemist to bring the two together," interjected Availia tiredly.

"Exactly right," responded Red. "So here is a lever that adds an element into the chamber," he instructed as he pointed to a red-handled lever.

"Here is another lever that adds the binding agent." He was now pointing at a blue-handled lever. "And here is quite a curious-looking knob, isn't it? This is for the alchemist to complete the reaction. The more you turn the knob to the right, the more of a reaction will take place, understand?"

Ethan looked puzzled, but nodded his head.

"This reaction creates extremely hot air — so hot, in fact, that it would easily catch anything on fire — I mean thousands of degrees of heat. So why doesn't the material that makes up the balloon portion catch fire?"

Ethan scratched his head. He had just wanted to know how the balloon could carry such a large ship around — and now he was worried about it catching fire. "Not sure," he replied.

"Well, how does your alchemy jacket work?" asked Red.

Ethan removed the glove from his left hand and showed Red his stone. "Still trying to figure that one out."

"Oh, you're a late bloomer, huh? How long have you had to carry that stone around? Two days? Maybe three," chuckled Red.

"Thirteen days," answered Availia.

Ethan slipped his stone back into the glove.

Red mouthed the words 'thirteen days' as he chuckled a bit more. "Wow … I mean, it'll happen, Ethan." Red winked at Ethan and gave him a slap on the back. "Think of this balloon as the largest and most expensive alchemy jacket you've ever seen. It's lightweight, and can hold extreme heat inside. And alchemy can also move her forward, back, up, down, left, right — you name it, she can do it."

"She?" asked Ethan.

"Well, yeah … it's a girl of course," said Red, looking over the rail. "There they are," he whispered, motioning Ethan to lean over the rail as well.

Ethan was not exactly sure who Red was talking about, but as he leaned over the rail he saw several hundred torches below.

"What is it?"

"That is Tirguard's army. Looks like they set up camp — I would guess they have three or so hours before they reach Losalfar. Which means they will most likely attack tomorrow," said Red quietly.

"There's a lot of tents down there," said Ethan.

"Tirguard has a big army. This isn't going to be easy — you sure you're up for it?" asked Red.

"I have to be," replied Ethan. "How long 'til we get to Losalfar?"

"It's right there." Red pointed across the front of the ship. "I'd say we will be there in less than an hour — you'd better wake your friends up, Ethan," added Red as he started pulling levers and adjusting knobs.

Ethan nudged Auren who had just begun to snore, and Availia went to the back of the ship to wake up Stanley.

"You'll all need swords with you, but it is only precautionary. Leave them to their sheaths unless you are provoked to do otherwise."

"But, I don't have a sword," complained Auren.

Red opened a horizontal compartment along the floorboards of the ship. Reaching inside, he quickly pulled out a rusty old sword that had lots of dings and dents in the blade. He tossed it over to Auren, who looked at it in disgust.

"What is *this?*" he complained.

"It's a sword," replied Red bluntly.

"But it's old and rusty," whined Auren as he felt the edge of the blade. "It's not even sharp!"

"It's all we got, kid. I'll have you know that sword was used back in the good ol' Stadion days — killed more men than any other sword you've seen in your life."

Auren appeared satisfied and shoved the sword through his belt like a makeshift sheath.

Ethan leaned over to Red. "Is that true?"

"No, I use it to anchor down the ship if I have nothing else to tie Gertrude down to," chuckled Red.

"Gertrude?" smirked Ethan.

"Yeah," answered Red. "Her name is Gertrude." He patted the rail of the ship as if it were his pet.

"Alright everyone, the torches are lit — meaning the welcoming party is present, prepare to disembark."

Red threw several levers and adjusted several knobs. The ship slowed and turned to the high walls of Losalfar. The platform was well-lit with torches and figures could be seen standing behind them. Ethan felt a slight bump that let him know the ship had landed. Red, meanwhile, jumped off, lashed down the ship and held the rope firmly.

Ethan, Auren, Availia and Stanley stepped off the airship one by one. Red nodded to Ethan, unlashed the rope, and jumped back on board.

"Good journey," yelled Red as a loud *whoosh* could be heard, followed by a flash of fire that could be seen through the open portion of the curtain.

The four stood on the platform, not entirely sure what was going to happen next. Ethan noticed the platform had designs carved in it and looked quite pleasant. Even the torches looked like a beautifully crafted version of Wegnel's miracle torches, with engraved metal and adjustable spindles.

"Now what?" whispered Auren.

"Not sure," replied Ethan under his breath.

A soft blue glow emanated through the shadows behind the lit torches. Ethan stepped forward, instantly recognizing the first Mitan he had ever seen in person.

"You're … Loka," stuttered Ethan. "I know you … I think."

"Correct," said the Mitan. "My name is Loka Tattur. You must be Ethan Wright. It is my pleasure to welcome you and your friends to Losalfar."

"Thank you," replied Ethan.

"And to what occasion do we owe this pleasure?" asked another figure that stepped from the shadow. This Mitan looked a bit different. He wore a black cloak, the hood not confining the soft blue glow that marked a full-blooded Mitan. His face was full of contempt, and his voice exuded disdain as if it pained him to be around Ethan.

"We came to warn you," said Availia in a rush. "Of … an impending attack."

"I am impressed on how well informed you all seem to be," said the strange Mitan. "But I have already informed Loka that we will be attacking this city at first light."

"And who are you?" blurted Auren.

"This is Ciprian," replied Loka. "He is here on behalf of the Aegis and the city of Gilfangir."

"And if I knew Ethan Wright were going to be here, my liege Xivon would be here to greet you. He is, after all, anxious to meet you in person, Ethan," smiled Ciprian mischieviously.

"But he is the most dangerous Mitan in the world, why would he be allowed in here?" asked Ethan.

Ciprian laughed.

"All are welcome here," replied Loka plainly.

"And that is what caused this mess to begin with," replied Ciprian under his breath.

Ethan ignored Ciprian's comment and looked back to Loka. "I think you misunderstand," explained Ethan. "Tirguard is on its way. They'll be here in the morning."

Loka remained calm and did not appear surprised. "That does complicate things a bit," he said.

"You see, Loka? It could not be any more perfect. We can unite our forces once and for all, and remove the humans entirely!" said Ciprian. "We do not have to fight each other, instead we can fight as one!" he bargained, leaning in to Loka.

"We will not join forces with you — we are not interested in the massacre of an entire race. Xivon's vision of the future is grim and will only put death on everyone's hands."

"It will be you or them, Loka. Think about it!" Ciprian spat on the ground, turned, and disappeared into the darkness.

"What was that about?" asked Auren.

Availia leaned in and gave Auren an elbow to the gut.

"What?" argued Auren.

"Shut up," hissed Availia. "You're being rude." She shot him a dirty look.

"He is with the Aegis — they have hunted and maimed humans since the last great war of Tirguard," said Loka. He looked at Ethan. "Your parents — they left Tirguard during that war. And since that time, it has never been the same here. The Aegis are Mitans that are beyond displeased that humans are in Tirguard. They, at one time, were okay with hunting down humans — but now … they have started creating traps with purposes of torture in mind. They wish to send a message with these devices — for humans to leave Tirguard and never return," he added, motioning them to follow him down a long staircase.

The four followed Loka down the staircase. They continued down a path that led through many tall trees, some of which had platforms high up in the branches. The platforms emanated with flashes of pristine blue, letting Ethan know that many Mitans were around. He knew he was being watched, but felt safe with Loka.

The city was indeed breathtaking, even when masked in darkness. Ethan felt at peace with himself — he had not felt this serene since he was with his twin brother.

To the right was a path that led to a long bridge that traveled across the middle of a pond, where Ethan could barely make out several structures in the darkness. They followed Loka down a path to the left and approached a grouping of gigantic trees that housed platforms about halfway up.

Ethan had never seen a tree dwelling until now. He looked up and saw that one of the platforms was still lit; it had to be at least fifty feet in the air. Loka led them up a staircase that encircled the tree in an upward spiral. Auren kept trying to wiggle the railing on his way up, to test the integrity of the structure. It seemed to pass his crude test, for he kept on climbing the staircase. They stepped onto the wooden platform and walked to the edge to look over the city.

"It is breathtaking, isn't it?" asked Loka.

"It's beautiful," replied Ethan. "Do you live way up here? I mean … is this your house?"

Loka gave a bit of a chuckle. "Some are houses, but these are the Watchtowers of old Aeroseth — so yes, you will be staying here tonight … it's safe up here," answered Loka. "The city was built from the ground up, which took hundreds of years. Every Mitan born of the city gives something back by adding to its beauty. The buildings, the statues, the bridge that passes over the pond, or simply the torch that lights our very conversation; all made by residents of the city, by hand, over time," added Loka with pride.

Loka put his hand on the railing and took a deep breath. As he spoke he had a look of despair on his face. "Before Losalfar stood, there was a grand city called Aeroseth. The city stretched as far as the eyes could see, even over what is now called Tirguard. But there always seems to be a need for war, and the time for Aeroseth had come. We won the war … if you would call it a victory. We successfully defended our city to the bitter end, and these Watchtowers are all that remain, holding strong on the city's edge. It was deemed a good defense for the heart of Losalfar as we rebuilt," explained Loka.

Ethan looked down at the railing he was leaning on. Even that had beautiful carvings of vines and leaves. He thought of what Aeroseth must have looked like and a warm feeling came over him. Loka seemed to sense this.

"That is why it is so unfortunate," said Loka.

"Unfortunate?" questioned Ethan.

"I know why you are all here. You need answers on a certain Stonewolf … and of course the whereabouts of Isaac Wright."

"Yes," exclaimed Ethan.

"Just as I wish I could show the four of you Aeroseth, I wish I had the answers you seek about your brother," said Loka as he put his hand on Ethan's shoulder. "I do, however, have information on the Stonewolf in our library — but now, I must make preparations for a war that I cannot possibly win. I will leave you with Ventu, my most trusted friend. He will show you a place to sleep — I will try and meet with you in the morning."

The Library of Truth

Loka was surrounded by one thousand Mitans belonging to the opposition. The one with the purple glow stood out among the others.

"Dregfin, this isn't the way to accomplish anything. I won't have any more Mitans die because of this," said Loka to the Mitan with the purple marking surrounding his left eye.

"I'm done talking, Loka, and … it was a mistake for you to come here alone," taunted Dregfin as he gave the signal for the Mitan force to attack.

Loka swiftly drew his sword, knowing that he had instructed his army not to intervene. The first Mitan came at him with a steady thrust. Loka easily avoided the thrust and countered by stabbing the Mitan in the foot. Immediately he had three more behind him — he disarmed the first and used him as a shield for the two remaining oncomers. He guided their swords, one into the Mitan-shield's leg and the other into the attacking Mitan's arm. Loka whipped around and knocked the third unconscious. Ten more Mitans came, followed by twenty more, and two hundred followed. Each one dropped, grabbing an arm or leg, but none being dealt a deadly blow by Loka Tattur. He fended one attack after another, until all nine hundred and ninety-nine Mitans under Dregfin's command lay on the ground, injured and in agony.

"You forgot one," said Dregfin as he drew his sword.

"I told you, no Mitans will die today — all of you are welcome back … always!"

Just then fire and ash, followed by black billowing smoke, shot out at Loka and filled the sky. Loka dashed to the side and drove his sword through Dregfin's hands, turning his opponent's blade on himself. The sword dropped to the ground — wisps of smoke were all that remained.

Ethan woke with a start as his heart raced. His breathing starting to slow, he sat up. He was used to waking up riddled in sweat. But this dream was different. It seemed to continue from when he had meditated in Edison's alchemy class. He wondered if the dreams were different because of his journey through the Oroborus. Regardless of the bad dream, Ethan felt rested and refreshed. Auren, on the other hand, was off to a slow start as he rolled over with the blankets covering his face.

"Are you getting up?" asked Ethan.

"Yew...." mumbled Auren.

Ethan went to the railing, leaned against it and looked over the city.

"Amazing," he said quietly to himself.

The city was quiet and almost serene. Ethan could see statues of heroic figures and buildings that paled in comparison to anything he had seen in Tirguard. He had thought nothing could top what a sight the city displayed at night. But in the daytime, its awe-inspiring grandeur passed before Ethan's eyes.

"Auren!" Ethan prodded. "Get up and look at this!"

"What? Who do you want, I mean...." Auren pulled the blankets from his head. "Oh — bright enough," he said in a tired voice.

He stood next to Ethan, looked around, shrugged his shoulders and went to get his things together. Ethan followed suit and they started for the stairs. The Mitan with the fierce blue markings, named Ventu, greeted them at the top of the staircase.

"It's about time, you missed breakfast. Here, I brought you these." Ventu gave them a handful of biscuits and some sort of leafy green vegetables.

"Thanks," said Ethan with a smile on his face.

Auren started chewing on the biscuits right away. He took a small bite at first, but immediately inhaled three more biscuits.

"Ventu, where are Stanley and Availia?" asked Ethan politely. Just then Availia came around the corner with Stanley following after.

"We made it to breakfast — you should have seen all the food they had!" exclaimed Availia.

"Food?" grunted Auren. "I like food."

"Fun feasting fresh fantastic food," exclaimed Stanley.

"Well you don't have to rub it in — anyways, these biscuits are really good," boasted Auren.

"We must be heading to the library if we are to meet Loka," said Ventu as he headed down the spiral stairs. "It's just over here." He pointed to a domed building with pillars lining the front opening.

"This place is great," said Availia as she walked inside.

There were no doors on the front, just an opening. The inner dome was painted with several marvelous yet scary creatures. Ethan nearly swallowed his own tongue when he recognized not one, but two of the creatures on the ceiling.

"That's the—" sputtered Ethan.

"The Stonewolf," finished Loka Tattur. "And I would guess that you recognize another up there?"

"Venenum Spiculum, or Dendrobates Azureus if you will," spouted Auren.

Ethan looked at Auren in shock, as did Availia, Stanley, Loka, and even Ventu.

"What?" complained Auren. "You know … the Ravim?" he continued. "WHAT? I have a thing for creatures, is all."

"He is correct," said Loka. "There are seven legendary creatures that represent each of the seven worlds. Each creature was known to demonstrate special abilities. Dendrobates Azureus, or the Ravim for example — is a heavily armored creature with unimaginable strength. It can burrow underground and chews on stone like butter. Lastly, it shoots spikes that can paralyze, poison, and even kill. If left undisturbed it is known to be rather docile and generally minds its own business. But you're not here about the Ravim, are you? You are here about the legendary lycanthrope, the Stonewolf."

"Docile?" exclaimed Auren. "Wegnel had us chasing this thing around his hut like a puppy!"

"Yeah, until the Stonewolf showed up," added Ethan.

"You had *two* legendary creatures facing you at the same time?" asked Loka curiously. "And you're still here to tell the tale?"

Ethan and Auren both nodded while Loka stood in disbelief.

"If you ever had a run-in with one of these creatures … well, you should be dead," said Loka, concerned.

"Ethan also faced the Stonewolf by himself at Tirguard," boasted Availia. "He scared it from the city completely."

"Well, maybe you're much further along than I thought."

"No, not at all," replied Ethan bluntly. "Wegnel helped us escape the first encounter — and I wouldn't have escaped the second, if it weren't for the fact that every time I grab onto a sword it seems to start things on fire. We really have no idea what we're doing, and no idea why this Stonewolf is after me. That's one of the reasons we're here."

"Well, one of the amazing things about this library is that everything written down is the truth," stated Loka, waiting for a reaction. Stanley's eyebrows rose slightly.

"You mean like the hidden records room in Tirguard?" asked Availia.

"Yes, exactly like that. That was the old library of Aeroseth. That room partially survived the war. Anything that is written here will disappear from the parchment if it is not true, and in some cases it will change to what is true."

"That's not how the room works in Tirguard. Anything that was written in one room seems to replicate into the hidden room," argued Availia.

"Oh … well then. Yes, because half of the building was destroyed in the war, disrupting the flow of alchemical properties that make the library work as expected."

"Alchemy?" asked Ethan.

"Yes, in fact — Wegnel helped us build this new library several hundred years ago, that is, before he was bound to the Oroborus. The goal is that you can not only learn by reading, but also by writing things down."

"Why did you have Wegnel help? Isn't there a more normal alchemist in Losalfar?" prodded Auren.

Loka chuckled. "Because Mitans cannot control alchemy like you — one of the many fascinating things about humans."

Auren grabbed some parchment at a nearby desk and started writing, then displayed his work to Ethan and Availia.

"'Auren Faryndon is the strongest boy alive,'" read Ethan aloud. "That is *really* funny."

"But a good test," added Loka as the ink started to fade away.

As the ink resurfaced, Ethan noticed the message had changed. Auren frantically tried to grab the parchment back from Ethan, but was unable to.

"What does it say?" asked Auren nervously.

"'Auren Faryndon is the strongest twelve-year-old human on this planet,'" read Ethan in disbelief.

"Yeah!" exclaimed Auren as he smiled from ear to ear.

"I could spend all day in here," smiled Availia.

"Me too," agreed Auren.

Ethan, on the other hand, immediately started writing on a new piece of parchment. He watched the words *'Isaac Wright is located nearby'* disappear from the page. New words did not appear in their place.

Loka placed his hand on Ethan's shoulder.

"I am sorry, Ethan, it doesn't work that way — and for that matter, it doesn't always work at all."

Ethan frantically started writing again, *'Isaac Wright is still alive'*. The ink once again disappeared from the page, and did not return.

"There are rules here that alchemy cannot defy. You cannot tell the future, only past events. You cannot see past events that are purposefully disguised in alchemy. And you cannot defy the will of the Oroborus — if the Oroborus does not wish you to see something, you will not be able to. I am truly sorry, Ethan."

Ethan was devastated. He laid the parchment on the desk and readjusted the pack on his shoulder.

"Well then … what do you have on the Stonewolf?" asked Ethan.

Loka smiled and grabbed a book from the shelf, handing it to Ethan.

"'The Seven Legendary Creatures, Their Historical Significance and Their Known Attributes,'" read Ethan out loud. "Can we borrow it?"

Loka nodded.

Ethan noticed Auren looking desperate and handed him the book. Auren immediately opened it and started reading.

Loka noticed Auren's enthusiasm and chuckled. "You can keep it. I will have my historians make me another copy."

Just then a Mitan wearing full armor walked into the library. He carried an interesting sword, which he handed to Loka. "Sir, here is what you requested. Also, we have spotted the enemy … it's time."

"That is, if there is still a library by this time tomorrow," added Loka as he smiled at the four. "It is time for you to leave now, Ethan Wright, Auren Faryndon, Availia Tanbe and Stanley VonHaven — it was my honor to meet you all. You are welcome back at any time. But before you leave, Auren … we have a gift for you."

A Change of Plan

"Can you believe this thing?" exclaimed Auren as he showed off his new sword. "Real Losalfarian steel!" he bragged as he struggled to lift the weight of the blade.

Ventu led them to the top of a great hill where they had a good view of Losalfar. The grass and thistle-wheat covered the slope of the hill as far as the eye could see.

Ventu showed Auren five discs that could be removed from the blade to lessen the weight of the sword. "You see — this way, as you get stronger, you can add weight to the sword and it will grow with you," instructed Ventu as he attached the five steel circles to Auren's sheath.

"We will rest here for a moment," interrupted Ethan.

"No," argued Ventu. "We cannot risk running into the Tirguard army, or any scouts from the Aegis army. I promised I would keep you safe — we need to keep moving."

"Running into the Tirguard army is exactly what we want to happen," challenged Ethan.

"Yeah, Ventu," added Auren. "We are here to stop a war — we're not going to let anything happen to you or your people."

Just then, loud bangs, flashes and rumbles came from the city of Losalfar. The Aegis army was placing the city of Losalfar under siege.

"I don't think you can prevent a war today," shrugged Ventu.

More rumbling could be heard, but Ethan could not tell where it was coming from. He turned and saw the massive and widespread Tirguard army heading right for them. Ethan watched as thousands strong marched toward them, carrying large royal blue and yellow banners.

Ventu, Availia, Auren and Stanley were now standing behind Ethan, staring at the massive army.

"There sure is an awful lot of them," said Auren as he sheathed his sword.

"Ngggu nggggu ngggu … yeah," agreed Stanley.

The army was approaching fast and Ethan could hear the footsteps marching in unison and the clanking of armor.

"I can't let you do this," pleaded Ventu.

The five of them paused, looked at the black-armored Aegis army attacking Losalfar, and back to the Tirguard army.

"Let me talk to them," asserted Ethan.

"You see, Ventu, what you need to know about humans is they are stubborn, and sometimes do stupid things," said Auren impertinently.

"If we can talk to them, maybe we can explain the truth," added Availia.

"Then you, my friends, would succeed in something that no man has done in over a hundred years," replied Ventu.

Ethan stood up straight and touched the hilt of his sword. "If they don't listen, then they can fight through me."

"Well in that case, I vote we go back to the city," said Auren in a smart voice.

Ventu paused for a moment, then looked Ethan in the eye. "Okay, Ethan … I am with you."

They walked toward the massive Tirguard army. Auren hesitated, and then with a reluctant shrug of his shoulders, followed the others. As they drew closer, a smaller group of men extracted themselves from the front line to greet them. The boys slowed their pace as they realized one of those men was none other than Heinrich Cornelius Agrippa.

"I see you have already found the time to become traitors, eh? Could not obey the laws I handed you, could not finish the classes — and now here … I … have caught you with this … Mitan," spat Heinrich. "Take him." Heinrich pointed to the Mitan, and two of the soldiers grabbed Ventu from behind and held his arms in place while a third took his weapons.

"Wait!" yelled Ethan. "You don't understand what you're doing!"

"I … Captain of the Tirguard armies, do not under—" Heinrich was cut off by another man.

"I am General Vacheal Lodbrok. I am in command of this army. Speak your side quickly, for I do not warrant a lack of haste at this time."

"General, the Mitan are a peaceful race. They had a civil war and are now plagued by a rogue group of Mitans that call themselves the Aegis. *They* are the ones attacking the people of Tirguard," disputed Ethan.

"You claim to know much for just arriving," stated the General.

"Yes, but it's the truth, I swear," exclaimed Ethan. "I also have this," added Ethan as he pulled a sheet of parchment from his pack and handed it to General Lodbrok.

The General looked it over and handed it to Heinrich.

"An order to cease our attack?" spat Heinrich. "From Edison Rupert?"

"He's a Captain of Tirguard," argued Ethan. "And no Tirguard army—"

"Will go into battle unless all Captains on the field agree to such a battle," interrupted General Lodbrok. "But Edison Rupert isn't on the battlefield, is he?"

"No sir, he sent us in his place."

Heinrich sneered.

"Is that it then?" asked the General.

"Well…." Ethan gulped.

The General paused and then looked over to Heinrich. "Get the men ready to move. Now."

"Wait!" exclaimed Ethan. "Sir, if you attack this city you will have to get past me," added Ethan as he stood ready.

"You'll have to get past *us*," added Availia, drawing her sword.

Auren nodded and drew his sword as well, as did Stanley.

The General held up a hand to halt the thousands of men that stood behind him. He looked Ethan in the eye, and then looked at the others who stood behind him.

"I appreciate what you're trying to do here, Ethan, brother of Isaac — you are indeed brave or incredibly stupid, but I am under direct order from the Castellan himself, civil war or not. I do not want to hurt such a noble young man as yourself," replied the General.

"Then sweep down and take out the Aegis first — the ones with black armor. At that point, if you still don't believe my words … then take the city," replied Ethan as he pointed to just east of the city, where the war was escalating. Catapults were raining down on the city and the Losalfarians were firing arrows at the oncoming Aegis.

The General scratched his chin and took a moment to think. He studied the two Mitan armies fighting below and then looked back at Ethan.

"Sir, if you sweep the center of the battlefield it will open our flanks to attack!" argued Heinrich frantically. "C'mon, he's just a stupid boy!" he snarled.

"And if both armies turn on us, what then, Heinrich?" snapped General Lodbrok. "Edison's students have a point that I cannot afford to ignore."

The General walked up to Ventu and got right in his face.

"If this is a trap, I will turn on the city immediately. Now then, give this *Mitan* his weapons back. You will fight right alongside me, so your city knows we are here together."

Ventu nodded.

"I hope you don't have any problems taking orders from a human."

"None, General," replied Ventu. "It's an honor to fight at your side."

"You bet it is," replied the General confidently.

He looked back over to Ethan. "Also, I won't have you or your friends getting involved in this battle, nor will I be responsible for your safety. The four of you go back to Tirguard — follow the trail we made, it should be clear," ordered the General.

"But, sir—" said Heinrich.

"Heinrich, move the men double-time, sweep the center of the black-armored soldiers," ordered the General.

Tirguard's army moved out, and the four companions stayed motionless as the river of men separated to move past them. Soldier after soldier passed Ethan, some purposefully bumping shoulders with him as they passed. The four stood and watched the massive army head down the hill and sweep around the walls.

"Well," said Ethan, "should we start heading back then?"

"Yeah," answered Auren.

Stanley nodded.

"You did a good job, Ethan," said Availia, smiling.

"I couldn't have done it without all of you."

"Did you see my spin move?" bragged Auren as he sheathed his new Losalfarian sword.

Ethan laughed, as did Availia. Even Stanley smirked a little as they started walking back to Tirguard. They followed the tracks of the massive army, which was not difficult at all.

Just then, Ethan heard a small *thump* at his feet. He looked down and saw that a black stone had come to rest just in front of him. He leaned down to pick up the stone and as he did, wisps of black smoke formed a dome around him. He dropped the stone and tried to jump backward, but could not move. Fog swirled and puffed all around him, slowly drawing into the wall so he could not see outside the sphere.

Ethan tried to look around, but his eyes would not move. He was frozen, looking straight ahead at grey and black billows of smoke. And just as in Ethan's dreams, the smoke formed into a face that was screaming — but no sound came. The screaming mouth opened wider and wider, until Ethan could see to the outside of the dome. It opened so wide that it made a doorway that a man could walk through.

And out of that doorway, a tunnel of smoke formed. At the end of the tunnel stood a sinister figure dressed in pitch black.

Ethan, held in place by some unknown force, stood there helpless and terror-stricken. He felt as if his hand should go for his sword, but instead it was frozen in time. He tried to move, but could not. He willed every last ounce of strength he could gather to move even a finger, but failed. He tried to scream, but was unable to do so.

Ethan's heart began to race — he was terrified of the figure in black. His heart beat faster and faster until the figure took a step toward him. Ethan's heart stopped when the figure's foot hit the ground. He began to panic. His nerves twitched and tingled. He wondered if this meant he was dead. All these years he had taken his heartbeat for granted, as he had never paid much attention to it — until it stopped.

A million thoughts raced through his head. The presence took another step toward him. He told himself he was only having another dream — he wanted to rationalize the cipher in front of him.

The figure raised its cowled head and wisps of smoke filled the doorway. It stepped through the fog. Again, Ethan tried desperately to move, but was unable to do so. The figure reminded Ethan of what death would look like — of what death would feel like. Fear took over every fiber of his being.

"I have so long waited for this moment," said the figure in a raspy whisper. Pale hands extended upward from the black robe and slowly drew back the long hood. Wisps of smoke rolled down the sleeves and coalesced into the sphere that imprisoned Ethan Wright. As the cowl drew back, a deep purple glow emerged. Piercing grey eyes, set in a pale face, revealed pleasure at having set such a successful trap.

The unnerving Mitan seemed well aware that his prey was unable to move. He stepped gracefully to Ethan's side, leaned into Ethan's ear, and whispered, "I am Xivon…."

Ethan's nerves felt as if they were on fire. He wished he could jump from his body and run. He wondered if his friends were trying to help him escape. And if they were, Ethan wished they would run instead — from what MacArthur considered the most dangerous Mitan alive.

"I wonder what one would have to say if this were his last moment," pondered Xivon as he walked behind his prey and peered down at Ethan's sword.

"Since you may not get the chance for last words, allow me to fill in the blanks." Xivon got right in Ethan's face. "Your brother is dead," said Xivon bluntly. "…I killed him," he added, looking deep into Ethan's eyes to see if he could find a reaction.

"I would bet that you want to grab that sword of yours and smite me with fire. But you cannot control it, you cannot wield it — it will not answer you, as … it is not yours," smirked Xivon as he tapped the top of the hilt with his fingers.

"So what is next?" he asked as he paced back in forth in front of Ethan. "Next … I am going to *kill* your friends outside as they stand motionless in time. And then … I am going to *kill* you." He turned his back to Ethan and drew a sword from his robe. It was long and thin like Ethan's, but the core was hollow except for a dim green glowing rod that ran almost the entire length of the blade.

"That is, of course, unless I can kill you now."

He turned and lunged the sword into Ethan's chest, but it halted before piercing the first layer of skin. A jolt of green light flashed outward, hitting the edges of the sphere and sending wisps of black smoke about. It pushed Xivon backwards several steps. For just a second Ethan thought he could see Auren through the smoke, as if frozen in time.

Xivon quickly sheathed his sword. He struggled for a moment, as if a price had to be paid for using the sword in that way, much like Ethan had experienced when his sword had burned him.

"You can't blame me for trying, it is, after all … part of the game — us being the most important pieces on the board," boasted Xivon with his raspy voice. "I've worked on this trap ever since you were born. It stops time for everyone outside the sphere — everything inside the sphere experiences time, but obviously, I am the only one able to move. If I had just a few more years … you'd be dead — just as well, I'll have to do it the old fashioned way. So then … Ethan Wright…." Xivon placed both his hands on Ethan's shoulders and stared him in the face. "Oh, your brother would be so proud of you right now — well then, are you ready to die?" He waited as if to get an answer from Ethan, but none came. "Let's not delay this Oroborus chess game any longer than needed."

Xivon pulled two more black stones from his robe and tossed them through the sphere on opposite sides of Auren, Availia and Stanley. He drew his sword with one hand and spit in the other. He picked up the black stone in front of Ethan and held it to his own mouth.

"Release," he whispered.

The black and grey fog swirled and gathered above Ethan's head. Suddenly, the smoke shot up into the sky with a loud *hiss*. The clouds overhead turned black and it started to rain. Xivon put the stone back in his pocket.

"Hey you!" yelled Auren as he drew his sword.

But it was already too late. A new trap was waiting behind Auren, Availia and Stanley. A gaping portal had formed between the two stones. It shimmered and rippled anytime a raindrop came into contact with it.

Xivon, out of Auren's reach, brought his sword far above his head. With the flat side of the blade, he slammed it to the ground with all his might. The blade curved until the tip slapped the ground, directing a shockwave at the three unsuspecting targets.

The massive shockwave ripped through the air with a loud *CRACK*, pushing Availia and Stanley through the portal. Auren hit the ground and rolled toward the opening with his free hand clawing at the ground, the other hand still grasping his sword — but he, too, slid through the portal.

Ethan's heart finally started beating, but his entire body, having undergone such duress, collapsed.

"DRAW YOUR SWORD!" screamed Xivon as he paced back and forth rampantly in front of Ethan. "Draw the sword that doesn't belong to you! DRAW IT!" he taunted.

Ethan could feel the blade tingling and crackling before he could even get his hand on it. He thought if he could pull the map from his jacket, he could use it to shield the heat like he had when he fought the Stonewolf. But he remembered that he had given it to Auren on the airship only the night before. Reluctantly, he reached for his sword. Scalding pain shot through his hand. He drew the blade just long enough to drop it in front of Xivon.

"Now then, Orobori … the game is over," spat Xivon with a malevolent smile.

He raised his sword and began to swing. A loud *CLANK* came, moments before Ethan's demise.

"Get away from him," yelled Auren, as he spun around, swinging his Losalfarian steel wildly at Xivon.

Xivon blocked the swing and grabbed Auren's alchemy jacket, which was clasped shut. Auren, in turn, grabbed a fistful of Xivon's cloak, along with a pendant that had flung its way out. The two were right in each other's face, separated by their swords, which blocked one another.

"Ah, son of a Faryndon — you managed to climb out of the hole that led to certain death, did you? I get to kill a Faryndon *and* Isaac's twin in the same *day?!* Well, this was certainly worth the trip up the hill," boasted General Xivon.

Xivon knocked Auren's sword to the side and lunged forward. His blade-tip pierced Auren's alchemy jacket and sank into his chest. Stunned, Auren's face contorted. Before he could move backward, Xivon whispered to his sword and a loud shockwave erupted that sent Auren flying. As he hit the ground, his shoulders plowed a deep furrow into the mud. The impact was devastating — as Auren's body lay motionless, his new sword lay abandoned in the mud several feet away.

The shockwave sent Ethan's hair blowing backward and he felt a massive pressure surge. Ethan felt like he was in the airship; his ears began to pop and his eyes to water.

He thought of how Auren had fought in the youth sword competition, how he had entered so he could stand up for Ethan, how the sword had broken in half from the force Auren used in his attack against Marcus. Scared and angry, Ethan knew this would be nothing like the contest.

"Now then, here is the death of Auren the so-called *mighty*." Xivon raised his sword and Ethan took a handful of cooling mud, relaxed his mind, and picked up his sword. He took two steps and did his best to block. The two swords collided and another shockwave sent Ethan stumbling backward. A loud *CRACK* echoed far down the hill. This shockwave pushed many soldiers off balance, and many more to the ground.

The mud in Ethan's hand was hardening and heat was blistering through. He took several steps backwards and raised his sword defensively.

"What do we have now? You found a way to hold onto the sword after all — for the moment anyhow."

The heat was bleeding through the cracks of the mud, beginning to burn his hand and arm. It was even making his face hot.

It was now or never. He pulled the sword back to deliver a wild swing, but it was too late. Xivon took a step forward and again slapped the flat of his blade to the ground with all his might. Again, the blade curved and connected with the ground, until the tip landed just shy of Ethan's feet.

The shockwave was massive. Ethan dropped his sword and fell to his knees. The pressure caved his ears, he could not hear or see clearly and his nose started to bleed. He was extremely disoriented —

he could not tell what direction he was facing and time stood still.

Ethan was alone. He decided he did not care what happened anymore. He could not find his brother, even if he was alive. His father was missing and his mother was dead. And now, his best friend lay motionless on the ground next to him. Ethan had failed them. He had failed everyone.

Blinded by tears, he knew the end was coming. He felt it, just like his brother had when the creature stood over him in Ethan's dreams. Then … he realized.

"My dreams," whispered Ethan to himself.

"It's time, Ethan," stated Xivon.

Ethan yanked off his glove and the stone with the missing chunk fell into a small mud puddle. It glimmered wetly. He was sure he had not picked the wrong stone.

"Three things to make a reaction," he muttered as blood from his nose dripped into the puddle.

He shoved his hand in the mud puddle, grasping the stone. It shook and vibrated wildly in his fist. His skin started to itch as stone formed on his hand and followed up his wrist. It continued up his arm, splitting the alchemy jacket from wrist to shoulder. The stone skin stopped short of his neck and chest.

He picked up the sword with his stone-skinned hand; with the other he clasped the top of his alchemy jacket. The rest of the clasps snapped shut from top to bottom. The garment reacted instantly to the heat coming from the sword, and the stone skin protected Ethan's hand and arm.

Xivon appeared to panic momentarily, but then came at Ethan with full force. Ethan swung as hard as he could. Molten fire shot from his sword, blasting out with such force that his boots sank into the mud. He leaned forward to regain his balance. The collar on his jacket rose higher to protect his face from the heat. The trail of fire streaked as far as the eye could see, over the soldiers fighting the war, past the city of Losalfar, and beyond the horizon.

Ethan released his grip on the sword, which was now chalk-white. Smoke billowed out from the sword and blew wildly in the wind.

The black fog in front of Ethan could only be the leftovers of General Xivon himself. It furled and twisted in front of Ethan, slowly forming into the same face that had appeared inside the dome, and inside Ethan's dreams. The mouth gaped open, as if to scream. Ethan gasped. He could not believe the fight was not over yet — but this time, he heard the scream.

"Tell the Castellan that I'm coming for his head!" shrieked the face as the fog roiled violently. The black smoke dissipated and blew away in the wind.

Ethan stumbled to his knees. Loka arrived to aid Ethan and

Auren. Ethan felt his hearing start to go. He saw Loka's mouth moving. He was saying something, but Ethan could not hear what it was. He fell backward, stared at the sky for a moment, and let darkness envelope him.

The Castellan's War

Ethan could not remember the ground being this soft. It felt like he was floating on a white cloud, made of feathers. Opening his eyes, he noticed the sun peering through a window and white sheets covering him. He realized he was no longer outside the city walls. He could still hear the ringing in his ears from the shockwave that had come from General Xivon's sword. He heard voices in the room. He focused his eyes and saw a Mitan nurse talking with Auren.

"Hey, you're awake finally!" said Auren, looking over from the bed next to Ethan.

Ethan smiled and struggled to sit up. "Where are we?" he asked in a groggy voice.

"I think we're in a temple — the hospital was full of the more seriously injured," replied Auren. "Mmm, the food here is great." He stuffed his face with bread and some kind of pudding. "You simply have to try some of this … stuff," he added, shoveling more pudding into his overflowing mouth.

"How did you survive? I mean … I saw him stab you."

Auren pulled the map from under his pillow and handed it to Ethan. Ethan smiled.

"That thing is wicked…," said Auren, "and maybe indestructible."

"I'm glad you're okay." Ethan was relieved. He quickly stuffed the map in his pack before anyone had a chance to come in and see it.

"Yeah, just got a sore neck, and this weird burn on my hand when I grabbed onto Xivon's robe. I think we solved our Stonewolf problem…."

He showed his hand to Ethan. The symbol that was blistered into Auren's hand matched the pinch-shackle.

"So *he* sent the Stonewolf to kill me?"

Auren nodded. "I must've grabbed his necklace when he shocked me with that weird sword of his."

"What happened to Availia and Stanley?" Ethan asked softly.

Auren put down his pudding and shook his head. He started to tear up and Ethan's stomach tied into knots as he assumed the worst.

"I'm not sure. The portal led to the edge of a cliff … I didn't see them anywhere," sniffled Auren.

Ethan did not know what to say. He stared down at his sheets.

"I was able to climb my way out and back through the portal. I heard wolves, Ethan. Lots and lots of wolves…."

Loka entered the room with his precise footing.

"Loka!" said Ethan. "Is Ventu alright? Did you talk with General Lodbrok?"

"Yes, Ventu is fine, and yes, everything is fine between us and Tirguard … thanks to you two and your friends," replied Loka softly. "I want you to know that I sent my best trackers to look for Availia and Stanley. Ventu personally volunteered," he added as he put his hand on Auren's shoulder.

"Ventu told me how you insisted that the Tirguard army listen to you or suffer the consequences," he chuckled.

"Yeah, Ethan, we would have showed them, huh?" added Auren, smiling.

"I met Xivon … up on the hill," said Ethan. "Or at least … I thought I did."

"A trap?" asked Loka, concerned.

"Yeah, I think we just destroyed the trap, I'm not really sure, but … I don't think Xivon was actually there."

Auren, too, looked concerned.

"Well, everyone at Losalfar saw you defeat Xivon. Even if it was just a trap, that's pretty good for a twelve-year-old alchemist."

Ethan looked down at his arm, which was a bit itchy and mostly still grafted with stone skin. He looked to the side of the bed and found his sword lying next to his pack.

"I had ten soldiers guarding your sword because it was too hot to carry. It took two full days to finally cool down enough to get it back here. It's actually still warm." Loka chuckled. "Now then, I think it's time you got some rest," he added.

"Ah, one last thing," said Ethan quickly. Loka turned back, waiting for Ethan to continue. "Um, Xivon told me this sword didn't belong to me."

"Indeed," answered Loka.

"Then how is it I came to find it? I mean, I pulled it from the alchemy vessel," asked Ethan hesitantly.

"This is no ordinary sword. That is, even if you're an *alchemist* you can't wield fire from just any blade. This sword was not made here — was most likely made in Contabesco. The sword belonged to another Orobori … Xivon's brother — Dregfin. When they decided to leave after the Aeroseth war to form the Aegis, they had a competition of sorts to see who would be the leader. After the city of Gilfangir was erected, Dregfin took his followers and led an attack on Losalfar in hopes of gaining the respect of the Aegis and becoming their new leader. At that time Losalfar was just being built as well, and since Aeroseth suffered such tremendous loss, he thought we would not have the resources to defend ourselves. He was mistaken — Dregfin was destroyed."

"By who?" interrupted Auren.

Loka seemed reluctant to answer. He looked over to Ethan with a nod.

"Loka destroyed him," answered Ethan. "He used Dregfin's own sword against him."

"Yes, but that was a long time ago." Loka nodded again.

"But how do *I* know that?"

Loka flipped over Ethan's stone-skinned hand, exposing the palm. Ethan looked. Inscribed in his hand was a serpent in the shape of a circle, eating its own tail.

"The tail-devourer has chosen you, Ethan. I imagine your dreams and visions are sometimes sent from the Oroborus. I think that is remarkable, and it says something about you," said Loka as he smiled.

"So what happened to the sword after that?" asked Ethan.

"We kept it here for many years — but we were afraid that it would not be secure. So it was placed in an alchemy vessel. The last I heard, it was owned by a man named Griswold Agrippa."

Both Ethan and Auren looked at each other in amazement.

"Now then, I think that is enough excitement for one day. Thank you, boys, for your bravery. I hope this will bring us closer to peace with Tirguard. When you feel better, I can escort you back, but please feel free to stay as long as you wish."

Loka took his leave. Drained, Ethan lay back down and relaxed his eyes.

"Hey, Ethan."

"Yeah?"

"Did you see that spin move?" asked Auren, chuckling.

Ethan smiled and nodded his head.

As the boys entered the city of Tirguard, they were greeted with a few looks of gratitude, but mostly sneering contempt from passersby. The great stone city had been plagued by murder, torture and fear, spread through the propaganda given by Tirguard itself. Inventions that did not support the anti-Mitan effort were melted down to become the boot heels of war, by order of past Castellans. Swimming in ignorance were the average townspeople, who may not have left the city in their entire lifetime, completely unaware that Losalfar was a peaceful city, and the Mitans that lived there were a peaceful group. And here Ethan and Auren had stood in front of a Tirguard-led attack that would have meant certain victory.

The City Watch that guarded the walls accosted Ethan and Auren with their eyes as the boys walked by. The boys did not say a word. They quickened their pace through the city in hopes that their presence would go unnoticed. But a familiar voice rang out from behind and stopped them in their tracks. It was Heinrich.

"And where do you think you're going? You two are coming with me!" he shrieked.

Heinrich muttered and swore under his breath as he led the boys into the throne room of Tirguard. The high walls were held fast by great stone pillars. Much like many buildings of Tirguard, the pillars were carved statues of armored men that appeared to hold up the ceiling. Ethan was amazed by the stonework before him. However, it was short-lived, as a massive voice echoed across the room.

"YOU STOLE MY VICTORY!" yelled the Castellan.

Ethan was not sure if the Castellan was yelling at him or at everyone in the room. Heinrich dragged the boys farther into the room, stopping in front of the throne. He then joined Tothyll, General Lodbrok, Edison and several soldiers who were standing to the side.

The weathered face of the stress-ridden Castellan was so used to giving orders that it looked more natural when yelling than when speaking normally. "Tell me, Ethan, is the Oroborus here to protect you, or this city?" asked the Castellan rhetorically.

"I don't know, sir," answered Ethan quietly.

"You don't know, eh? Well the report that was handed to me is that Losalfar still stands. Is that true?"

"Yes, sir."

Several attendants stood next to the throne where the Castellan was sitting. One leaned forward, offering a plate full of grapes and other fruits. The Castellan waved him off.

"I sent these men … MY MEN … to sack that city … and you choose to sabotage them?! To what end? To play in this Oroborus game of chess and kill some Mitan that doesn't bother me in the slightest?"

"I didn't kill anyone, sir," stated Ethan, suddenly distracted by

Tothyll's flashy jewelry. One of the necklaces had a pendant in the same shape as the symbol on the pinch-shackle, and that of Xivon's necklace. He gave Auren a sharp elbow in the ribs.

"Ow, what?" whispered Auren out of the side of his mouth.

Ethan motioned over to Tothyll.

"Look at Tothyll's necklace, it matches the burn on your hand," whispered Ethan.

Auren just about jumped out of his shoes, but quickly contained himself as the Castellan stopped his rant for a moment.

"I'm sorry, is there something more important you would rather discuss?" asked the Castellan smartly.

"No, sir," said both Ethan and Auren.

"As I was saying — I have over a thousand men that say otherwise. They saw you use alchemy and obliterate a Mitan named Xivon. I must say, since you stopped me from destroying that city, it was the *least* you could do, killing its leader."

"Xivon is not of Losalfar, he's the leader of the Aegis … from Gilfangir. And I didn't actually kill him, it was a trap that I destroyed."

"And how do you know he is not dead?"

"Because—" Ethan decided he would try and keep his mouth

closed.

"I'm not in the mood for games, boy, TELL ME!" commanded the Castellan, as his voice boomed through the hall.

"Because after I destroyed the trap it told me it was coming … for your head … sir," said Ethan reluctantly.

The Castellan slammed his fist on the arm of the chair and stood up. Ethan jumped back a bit, as did Auren. The Castellan's face turned as red as a tomato.

"You mean to THREATEN ME IN MY OWN CITY!" screamed the Castellan.

His voice echoed off the walls, pillars and ceiling. No one moved, and a long moment of awkward silence ensued.

"Castellan, sir, if I may." Edison stepped forward.

"NO YOU MAY NOT!" boomed the Castellan.

Several moments passed before the veins started to settle in the Castellan's head and neck. He sat back in the throne and calmly continued.

"Ethan Wright, you and your friends participated in treasonous affairs. As a consequence, you lost half of your party — I have no doubt that you feel this is punishment in itself. However, as of now, it seems I have no choice but to close down the alchemy school once again. I believe the will of the Oroborus is to keep you safe — that does not include you leaving the city and mingling in diplomatic affairs."

The Castellan then noticed Ethan's ripped alchemy jacket. "What's that on your arm, some kind of alchemy *magic?*"

Ethan quickly put his arm behind his back, as if to hide his stone skin. But just then, the doors of the throne room slammed open and fully armored soldiers marched inside in a double line. The pairs split off so that a full line of soldiers were on either side of the room. The Castellan shot up out of the throne.

"No, no, Castellan — please have a seat … and finish your speech. I was enjoying the part where you think Ethan ruined your chances for success," stated King Basileus.

"My Lord, what are you doing here?" asked the Castellan.

"I read a full report as I came through the Oroborus. I guess I am here to check on the initiation of a war that I did not authorize."

"Well we had an opportunity to defeat the Mitans once and for all … there was no time to—" stuttered the Castellan.

"No time to send a messenger?" asked the King. "Hmm … a lesson then, in humility, Castellan — I think is needed. Everyone follow me outside to the courtyard, now!"

The King walked back through the doors and everyone followed him outside, including the Castellan. Hundreds of townspeople were gathered in the square, full of speculation and gossip. The King raised one of his hands and quieted the crowd.

"We all stand on equal ground today, as this is not our world. We are guests here. And as guests, we wish to leave a good impression on our hosts. It cannot always be done, but we must try just the same — so I ask today," announced the King as he paced back and forth with his hands behind his back.

"General Lodbrok," said the King loudly.

"Yes, Sire." The General stepped forward with his chin held high.

"Tell me what happened yesterday, General," instructed the King.

"I was ordered to sack Losalfar, Sire. I then met Ethan Wright and his friends on the cusp of the battlefield. He told me that Losalfar was split in two — and had entered into a civil war. The faction at Losalfar is peaceful. The faction known as the Aegis are the ones responsible for attacking our citizens," answered the General.

"And?" asked the King.

"And what, Sire?"

"Do you believe Ethan?"

"I have no reason not to, Sire," answered General Lodbrok as the crowd booed and jeered. "I fought alongside the Mitans to defeat the Aegis, Sire. Their cause is worthy, and they are honorable people."

The crowd started to quiet down, but chatter could still be heard.

"Anything else?" asked the King.

The crowd became completely silent.

"Yes, Sire. Had I ignored Ethan's plea and attacked Losalfar anyway, both armies could have turned on us and thousands of human deaths would have resulted."

"There, my Castellan. You have your war … against the Aegis. And because of Ethan Wright and his friends…," announced the King as he motioned for the crowd to part. Ethan just about jumped out of his alchemy jacket as he saw Availia and Stanley walking toward them, with none other than Ghislain and Odin behind them. "…we now have an ally — the city of Losalfar."

Ethan and Auren, grinning, ran over to greet Availia and Stanley with excited chatter and hugs. The crowd cheered and Edison Rupert smiled and went over to meet the students he feared he had lost. He shook Odin's hand and greeted Ghislain.

"Odin, Ghislain … what took you? You left before I did," said the King

"The Oroborus known as Cabra sent us to the wrong place,"

answered Odin, smiling. "And by some coincidence, we bumped into Availia and Stanley."

Stanley leaned into Ethan's ear and whispered something. Ethan stood in shock as he looked at Stanley.

"But you didn't—"

"I know, Ethan. I have no reason to stutter — not now or ever again," replied Stanley, as he pointed directly at Tothyll. "It was him that did this to me — in an experimental alchemy class, long ago. And Odin and Ghislain said he's the one—"

"Behind the Stonewolf," interrupted Ethan and Auren.

"MacArthur said that no *one* man could control a creature like this. Which means there had to be *two* of them that controlled the Stonewolf," said Ethan precisely.

"What?" asked Availia.

"When Auren and I fought Xivon — Auren grabbed his necklace and was hit with that strange sword," he said, as he grasped Auren's wrist and thrust the burnt hand in Availia's face.

The mark that was burned into his palm showed plain. Ethan pulled the pinch-shackle from his pack and matched the symbols.

"It would take more than one person to control a legendary creature. Tothyll has a matching necklace," stated Ethan.

The King smiled as he overheard the young alchemist's detective work come to fruition. He signaled his Guard toward the over-dressed criminal. Tothyll, noticing the momentum turning against him, turned on his heel and ran. He was immediately detained by none other than Heinrich.

"And where is it you think *you're* going?" said Heinrich coolly, as he firmly pressed his sword tip to Tothyll's chest and then up through the necklace in question.

As the guards detained the prisoner, Heinrich tore the necklace from around Tothyll's neck. The soldiers then escorted Tothyll to the King. The King again raised his hand and the crowd of townspeople immediately quieted down.

"Do you have anything to say for yourself?" asked King Basileus.

"I have served your kingdom faithfully, my Lord. You couldn't possibly believe these *students* over me?" begged Tothyll.

Stanley pushed forward and got in Tothyll's face. "My name is Stanley VonHaven of the VonHaven estate. The alchemical properties that you experimented with — the ones that made me stutter and live in a fog for all these years — expired when Xivon sent me through the portal. I know everything you've done, Tothyll … and I have quite a story to tell," said Stanley boldly.

Tothyll was enraged. His face twisted and his eyes grew large, as if a completely different man possessed him. He struggled to leap toward Stanley and Ethan, but was restrained by the guards.

"I'LL KILL YOU!" he screamed. "I'LL KILL YOU ALL!"

"Looks like we got the right man then," stated the King. "Oh, and Whitehaven is great at academics, agriculture, and even has terrific blacksmithing — but … we're still working on our quality stonework — keep that in consideration for the next story you make up," smiled the King as he signaled the guards to take the prisoner away.

"Castellan! Keep this traitor in prison until Tirguard is no more, or until death takes him and then some. Speaking of prisoners — release MacArthur … it seems we have a reliability problem with the other Oroborus — what's its name … Cabra? We will need Wegnel MacArthur more than ever … with his Oroborus … Dimon."

The Castellan nodded subserviently, and with a disgusted look upon his face he nodded to Heinrich to secure MacArthur's release.

The King raised both of his hands and addressed the townspeople. "The Curse of Silence has ended," he announced proudly. "Enemies who wish to reveal themselves will do so, in order to stop mankind from coming through the Oroborus into Tirguard. We will squander those proceedings with a solid defense of negotiation and great stone walls. We will not falter … we will not run … but above all, we will not sacrifice a chance for *peaceful* co-existence, or deprive ourselves of peaceful exploration in faraway lands. Mankind is curious," he added as he looked over to Ethan, Auren, Availia, and Stanley. "This curiosity will get us into trouble at times, but stand united and we shall remove ourselves from these troubles. Stand united … and we will not fail!"

The crowd applauded and cheered. Ethan could hear his name being chanted. He wished his brother was with him to share in the celebration, but he was happy just the same to be with his friends.

As the cheering continued the King shook Ethan's hand and pulled him closer.

"You did me a great courtesy, Ethan, and I can't wait to see what you do next," said King Basileus graciously. He put his hand on Ethan's shoulder and smiled. "Oh, and I would very much like to see this airship of yours!"

NOTE FROM THE AUTHOR

Dear Reader,
Thank you for reading Ethan Wright and the Curse of Silence. I've had a great time writing my novels and hope you've had a great time reading them. I will always put forth my best efforts to bring you the best content imaginable.

Thanks!

Kimbro West

You can learn more about the Author by visiting www.kimbrowest.com
Thanks for reading!

www.ingramcontent.com/pod-product-compliance
Lightning Source LLC
LaVergne TN
LVHW091027080826
845145LV00002B/385

* 9 7 8 0 9 8 8 7 8 7 0 1 8 *